A
SILENT
PROMISE

A
SILENT
PROMISE

Namrata Gupta

Srishti
PUBLISHERS & DISTRIBUTORS

SRISHTI PUBLISHERS & DISTRIBUTORS
Registered Office: N-16, C.R. Park
New Delhi – 110 019
Corporate Office: 212A, Peacock Lane
Shahpur Jat, New Delhi – 110 049
editorial@srishtipublishers.com

First published by
Srishti Publishers & Distributors in 2015

*To my family, whose thumbs up
every time I wrote a chapter,
made me write even more.*

Red and White

I was climbing up the stairs with someone. I don't know who that person was. I looked to my left, but all I could see was tall red walls with magnificent architecture. I looked straight ahead. I could see a chamber with white walls, a white ceiling and a white floor. Red and white were the only colours I could see around, like a newlywed bride who focuses incessantly on her bangles of the same colours, carrying with them dreams for the future. While the two of us walked up the stairs, heading towards the chamber, something was stopping me from seeing his face. All I could figure out was his black coat, black tie, white shirt and black pants. His face was blurred, just like the surroundings. Everything was hazy. Like the vision of a person who wasn't wearing his high powered spectacles. Suddenly he took my hands in his and looked at me. A feeling of warmth, love and compassion ran through my heart like blood through veins. I still couldn't see him, but I got the feeling that I didn't need to. That touch, that feeling was what I knew, what I trusted. We walked inside the chamber and I ran towards the balcony. The doors leading towards the balcony were open. I took a deep breath and felt the lovely soft breeze. I examined the architectural design of the walls very closely. I wanted to imprint them on my mind. I could envision how someone standing outside would see me... as a woman standing in the balcony of the Red Fort. Suddenly I could see the big picture. It was the Red Fort.

I heard a voice. I looked back, but it was dark. I could see a shadow trying to break us apart and take him away from me. I kept trying to hold on to his hand, but was overpowered. I could see him receding into the abyss of darkness and tears rolled down my cheeks with each step he took away from me. I tried to run into the darkness but it was repelling me, making me feel helpless. I saw the darkness coming towards me as if to swallow me. I was shouting and screaming when suddenly I heard...

"Wake up! Wake up!"

Someone was shaking and tickling me.

"You are late. Wake up!"

It was my mother.

"Mom! I dreamt about it again!" I said.

"You are just imagining things. Come on now! Get up! You are already late. Don't think about that. It was just a dream. The more you'll ignore it, the better you'll feel," she replied

It was my third day of college. As a fresher, the first two days hadn't gone too well as I was in no mood to have fun. I would go to college unwillingly. I had recently broken up with the love of my life. I could think of nothing but him. I had made a few friends in college, but not many. Being an introvert and not being a huge fan of talking incessantly, I never had many friends anyway.

Our driver dropped me to college every day, and that day was no different. After entering the college, I headed for the notice board. One of the recent notices stated that the first year students had to go to the library to collect their provisional library cards. I did as instructed. After standing in the queue for an hour, which seemed more like an eternity, the librarian asked, "Course?"

"English Honours," I replied

"Admission Number?" he asked.

"It's 5032," I replied

"Avantika Sareen?" He asked

"Yes."

He handed over to me the four library cards with 'Hindu College, University of Delhi' written on them.

I was late for my class, thanks to the queue; the teacher allowed me to get in, thanks to it being just the third day of college.

Struggle

Some hope held together by a string of imagination,
Some wishes keeping me alive with an aroma of expectation.
We facing the world together is the only thing I once believed,
Without you it has been ages since I've existed and not lived,
Every hour, every minute, every second when I breathe,
A bunch of memories of pain and anguish I wreathe,
Wouldn't God scorn at the idea of separating two souls and use his power,
Or will I have to lie in my grave without receiving from you, some flowers?
Is this the way by which happiness of my life would end,
Or will I receive with this pain, laughter to blend?
The great lovers of this universe have never been together,
But didn't you say that our love was forever?

You never meant a word you had said and always lied,
I've paid the price of trusting you and every night I've cried.
I know our souls are very far away, yet it feels so near,
I've already lost you, then why this fear?
When I got you, I felt like a princess without having been crowned,

With the solemn pledges of love, weren't we bound?
I loved you so much, yet you put me aside,
And this is how the scars of your love leave me,
Smiling from outside but dying from inside.

Every night I used to read this poem I had written not long ago; it reminded me of what I had lost.

A month had passed since I had heard from Aarav, my love, and two weeks since college had started. In these two weeks, I had done nothing besides weeping and writing poems. While the others were busy finding new boyfriends and girlfriends, I was waiting for Aarav to come back. I didn't like to stay in college for long hours, though I always checked Aarav's last seen on WhatsApp every hour. Being at home made me feel closer to him. Perhaps because he lived close to my house. I hoped every day that he would come back, but deep inside I knew that he wasn't a one-woman man.

Since, these were the initial days of college, we didn't have many classes to attend. Irrespective of what class I attended, I could concentrate only for the first fifteen minutes.

I found one of my professors very cute, but then, it was not love. There were many boys in my college whom I liked but then again, it wasn't love. I didn't hang out much during those two weeks, for I had no good friends till then. It was also due to the eagerness of reaching home early so that I could take off the cover of the smiling face hiding my sadness. I had visited the Kamla Nagar market once though, a must visit for the students of North Campus of Delhi University, but only to buy books.

It was Monday again. In order to hide my poems from my mother, I used to keep them in my college handbag. I put the recent one in my college register.

"Hey Avantika! You left this," Anamika said.

Anamika, Ritvik and Manvika were the people with whom I bonded well. Anamika was holding out a sheet of paper. She handed it over to me. It was my recent poem.

"From where did you get this?" I asked and was embarrassed at the thought of her having read its contents.

"It had fallen down when you were taking your register from me. I noticed it later. It is good by the way. I like the way you write. You never told me that you write poems too."

"Oh yes, I do. Thank you," I said.

"Wow! I write poems too. By the way, may I know whom is it addressed to?" she asked.

"Nobody. I was just getting bored so I wrote it. Nothing serious," I replied, folding the paper and trying to divert her attention towards her crush. She was single.

"Look he's coming. Right behind you," I said.

"Don't change the topic. Come on! You can tell me. Who's he?" she persisted.

"Nobody," I replied.

"Really?" she asked.

"Okay. I had a boyfriend. We broke up. I got emotional thinking about the past one day and wrote it."

"You loved him?" she asked.

"Yes," I replied, clearing my throat.

"Awww. Don't worry. We'll look for a new guy for you. Come, come. Forget that jerk."

I smiled and went with her. From that day, we got really close.

Endearment

Visiting Aarav's Facebook profile was like my daily pilgrimage. That one night was no different. It read:

'Aarav Sharma was tagged in a video' – 2 likes.
'Aarav Sharma added a new photo' – 23 likes.
'Aarav Sharma was tagged in a photo' – 16 likes.

He had ten subscribers, five subscriptions and thirty-eight profile pictures. Suddenly, a chat box popped up on my screen interrupting my 'investigation'.

Hey! We were in the same school at some point of time, right? It said.

I had recently added a guy named Rohit on Facebook. It was him.

Hey! Yes, we were. You shifted to some other school later, right?

Yes. I went to DPS Mathura Road.

Oh great! So which college? I typed.

Hindu. What about you?

Whoa! I'm in Hindu too. Which course?

Economics Hons. Never seen you in college. Which course are you in?

English Hons, I replied.

Where do you put up?

Defence Colony. What about you?

Hauz Khas.

Oh! Okay. Which stream were you in?

Science. And you? he asked.

Me too. So, you too weren't interested in Science courses like me? :-P I typed with a smile on my face.

Nopes. Economics interested me more.

Cool! ☺

We should meet up in college some day.

Something felt right about this chat, about him. He had a nice DP too!

Yeah..We will :-D I typed. My face was brimming with happiness by then.

How will I contact you? Can I have your digits?

We exchanged numbers.

I gotta go now. Feeling sleepy. Catch you later. Good night. I wrote.

Sure. Good night.

I don't know why but I was kind of looking forward to meeting him. Somewhere deep inside, I felt that this was the universe telling me that I should move on. That probably explains why I couldn't sleep that night.

●

The next day, I was dressed in my best. I wore my favourite blue and black top with blue jeans. I didn't walk around much in college lest I displeased my very well combed hair. It was 10.30 a.m. when I received a text message from him. I had been waiting for it since 8.00 a.m. I was in a very boring class at that time and he had asked me to come to the canteen.

I'm in a class right now. Can't we meet around 12:15? I've two consecutive classes of the same teacher actually. I replied in an instant.

I am going home in an hour. Came his reply.

Huh! Can't he wait! It was his mistake! If he had texted earlier, I would've never gone for that boring and irritating class.

Hey! My teacher has just announced that he will give us a break in between. So, as soon as I get free, I'll come. Wait there only. Ok?

Why can't you come now? he asked.

Coz I'm in the class. Dumb question!

As soon as I replied, the break was announced. I asked Anamika to come with me.

"I've to go and see a guy," I said.

She readily agreed.

"Sir, can we go get something from the canteen?" I asked my teacher since he didn't seem to have any intention of leaving the room.

"Okay. Come back in ten minutes," he said.

Yippie! I called Rohit.

"Hey! Where are you?" he asked.

"I'm just coming in two minutes," I said and hung up.

I had seen him in school as a fat nerdy kind of a guy with weird hair. When I reached the canteen, I looked everywhere. I noticed a guy in a white shirt and blue jeans who had turned around in his seat. I knew it was him. His face had changed since I saw him in school. He was sitting there with his friends. All of them were smiling, chatting and having fun, but he was serious. That seriousness was kind of adorable. I fell in love with him when I saw him. I had fallen for him – for the glow of his face, for the seriousness of his looks, for the fact that only seeing him made me feel secure.

I had not even started a conversation with him. I didn't even know how he was. But I knew that if you start feeling comfortable by just looking at somebody, without even knowing them to a considerable extent, it means something.

I walked towards him. He saw me and stood up. He left the company of his friends and walked towards me. As we were walking towards each other, I could tell a lot about him just by looking at the way he walked, his fashion sense and the confidence that was oozing out of him. I didn't want to seem over anxious but didn't know what to do. I started framing our conversation in my mind and got carried away. It was only after I heard his voice that I got back to reality.

"You're Avantika?" he asked.

"Yes," I replied.

"Look at you. All slim and handsome," I added jokingly.

He blushed. I smiled.

"Come. Let's sit somewhere," he said.

I followed him. He met a friend on our way to the sitting area and they started chatting.

"Avantika!" Anamika called out, pulling my arm.

"Where are you lost? I asked you so many times if he was Rohit when he was coming towards us but you never replied!" she scolded.

"Sorry! I didn't hear you," I said. I was blushing!

"Didn't hear me? Really? If I would have any been louder, the whole college would've heard me. Leave it! Okay now, tell me what am I supposed to do? Give you company or leave? I know you aren't going to attend the next class," she winked.

"Shut up and come with me," I said.

Soon, Rohit was back with us and we found a place to sit. I sat facing him.

"So she's your friend?" he asked.

"Yes, she's Anamika," I replied.

"Okay. So how's the crowd of your class?" he asked. And like that started a question and answer round. Anamika eventually went away to attend the class and I was left alone with him. I didn't want to bore him so I kept on asking questions to keep the conversation lively. As per the answers I received, he wanted to enjoy college and get good grades too. He couldn't compromise on his studies. He seemed to be a serious guy. A guy who could be trusted, who was responsible and knew what his limits were.

I had thought that I wouldn't attend the class but Rohit left early. He had to go somewhere. Having nothing else to do, I was heading towards the class when I encountered Nisha. Nisha was my classmate and we were good friends. I had always thought that she was a nice girl but appearances are deceptive. Very deceptive.

"Hey! Not attending the class?" she asked.

"I am on my way to the class," I replied.

"I saw you with that guy. Who's he?" she pointed her finger towards him.

"My schoolmate," I replied.

"Schoolmate or boyfriend?" she interrogated.

"Schoolmate. We've met for the first time after many years," I replied.

"You're single, right? Why don't you go for him?" she questioned me.

I just smiled.

"Come on! You can tell me," she continued.

"We'll see. We've just met. Let's see," I said, hesitatingly.

"Oh! So you're interested?" she winked again.

"Yes," I said, thinking that there was no harm if I told her.

"Great!"

Though late, we were allowed to enter. Anamika kept looking at me throughout the class though we were sitting at the opposite ends. She was sitting on the first seat of the row on the right hand side while I was being LLB, i.e. Lord of Last Benches, on the left hand side.

"You came back quite early," Anamika said after the class.

Thank god Manvika and Ritvik were absent that day. Otherwise, I would have died answering their questions.

"He left. He had to go somewhere," I said.

"Stupid boy! He should've spent more time with you," she said.

"Hmm..."

"What did you talk about?" she asked.

I told her about some parts of our conversation. He had one girlfriend in the eleventh grade and he didn't love her. He's single. Blah... Blah... Blah!

I kept wondering on my way back home whether he had liked me, whether he thought of me as a good girl or a bad one, etc. It was as if I had acquired a sudden lease of life. I had been led out of my narrow minded thoughts of Aarav and had been given eyes to look around and acknowledge that there was still a lot to be done apart from brooding over Aarav!

When I logged into Facebook after reaching home, I received a notification saying Rohit had liked my profile picture. I took it as a response to our meeting. Maybe he liked meeting me! Being sure of my fondness for him, I returned the gesture by liking his profile picture too! That's the new way of getting the message across, I guess. But contrary to my expectations, the story ended there. I had expected him to start a conversation with me about our meeting or something else, but he didn't. Well, nor did I!

Betrayal or Misunderstanding?

Three days had passed. Rohit and I had not spoken at all after the meeting. We would see each other in college and wave to each other, but that was pretty much it. We would sit in the canteen with our friends and keep looking at each other after short intervals, but would pretend that we were too busy to notice. Anamika had advised me to initiate a conversation with him and I had made up my mind to do so until I saw him with a girl in Kamla Nagar market. Though she was not at all pretty and was probably a friend, I was much displeased and was reluctant to take the first step towards starting a conversation with him.

When we were going for our class after a break that day, I saw Nisha sitting on one of the seating walls.

"Hey!" I greeted her.

"Hey!" she said back.

"You know what! That guy whom you met a few days back sent me a friend request on Facebook."

I was confused. I didn't know who she was talking about.

"Who?" I asked.

"What was his name! Umm..Ya...Rohit," she answered.

I was shocked. Rohit. What? When? Why? How?

"Do you know him?" I asked.

"No, I don't know how he found me. He might have seen me with you some day in college,"she said.

I could not believe it, but it was a lesser shock than the one I received after that.

"He has even asked me to meet him today," she continued.

Whaaattt? I was completely taken aback.

"So you're going to meet him, eh?" I tried to retain my composure while asking that.

"Obviously not! I know you like him. I can't do this to you. You can trust me. You are a good friend," she proclaimed.

Phew!

"That's very sweet of you, Nisha. But if you want to meet him, then go ahead! He has asked you himself. It's entirely your choice. Don't worry about me," I said.

"I know you like him and that is what matters. Now, leave the topic. Let's go to class. We're getting late," she said.

"Ya...okay! Thanks for doing so much for me," I said, being overwhelmed by her sweet gesture.

"No problem," she said.

I kept wondering how Rohit came across Nisha the entire day. I came to the conclusion that he must have seen some of her pictures with me in my profile and perhaps had liked her in them. Or, he could just be trying to make new friends in college. That's all.

The next day Nisha told me that she was in college till rather late and had encountered Rohit. They had just said 'hello' to each other. Though this encounter was short, it had made me a little hopeless about Rohit and me. As a result, I started missing Aarav again and that too, more than before.

It was not as if he was out of my mind since the day I had met Rohit. I had always been keeping an eye on him on Facebook, but the intensity of checking in on him had reduced in the past few days. Unfortunately, it came back to square one.

Rohit and I had not encountered each other for about three days in college. It was almost a week after Nisha and he had started talking when Nisha told me that Rohit had asked her to accompany him for a movie. I was now sure of his fondness for her. I, of course, felt bad because Rohit had been my only hope after Aarav, but I still congratulated her and told her that she could date him if she wanted to as I had no feelings for him whatsoever. But deep inside, somewhere I had the feeling that this couldn't happen. Firstly, I was not at all convinced that Rohit could ask her for a movie in such a short span of time as he seemed to be a really serious guy when I met him. He was clearly focussed towards his studies, not girls. Secondly, I had seen Rohit with his friends while I was with Nisha and he hadn't even waved to her. Well, nor me. Perhaps, he didn't like to wave to girls in the company of his friends. God knows! Thirdly, I had not seen them talking to each other in college ever. If they had been so engaged with each other that he had asked her for a movie, then I should have seen them talking to each other in college at least once. And also, being objective, she was not that pretty to drive him this crazy.

Nevertheless, I was now completely hopeless about my future with him.

I wanted Aarav...needed him...to comfort me...badly... very badly! I was ready to give away anything to make him come back to me but I knew very well that he was a spoilt guy.

It was nearly the end of August. The days passed. Rohit and I had started ignoring each other. We didn't even greet each other if we happened to pass by. We became strangers…strangers who happened to know each other till some time ago…like me and Aarav. On one such day, I was sitting in the canteen with my friends when I saw Rohit with his group of friends. He was quiet, just like the day I had seen him in the college for the first time. He seemed innocent and I had a soft corner for boys who looked innocent. I had always fallen for those who looked innocent. A boy with green eyes, an extremely fair complexion and a great personality but with no sincerity wouldn't interest me more than the one with average but innocent looks. Aarav seemed very innocent when I had fallen for him. My earlier crushes too had the same quality.

Perhaps, it was because they appeared like poor dove-like creatures in this mean world full of beasts. But trust me, I was the only one who got tamed by these so called 'dove-like creatures'. Huh! Maybe I could connect with them because I was innocent too. A shy person cannot stand up to a person who speaks very loudly, is authoritative and has more people to support him in a fight, for example. He would rather give up than argue with such a person in public even when he knows that he's right. Sometimes, I wished I was not shy, for being quiet and shy was sometimes a curse, because people would never let you take the credit of doing something good. Ultimately, to get the credit, you'd have to change yourself a little, which implies, losing a part of yourself to get your place in the world – a major tactic to survive in this Big Bad World.

"Hey! Where are you lost?" Manvika asked.

"Nowhere," I answered.

"Look! There's Karan," Anamika cried.

"He's the President of Dramatics Society, right?" Manvika asked.

"Yes, he is. He is hot!" Anamika drooled over him.

"I find most of the boys of Dramatics Society hot. It seems as if the major chunk of hotness of our college is in there," I said.

"Oh yes. I like Rahul too," Anamika said.

"He's cute!" Manvika winked.

Rohit and his friends were still sitting there but we had a class so we left. As I climbed up the stairs and moved to go towards the right, a tall handsome man came in front of me. He smiled and moved towards my left. He limped but he was really tall! Around 6'2" or 6'3"!

"Hey! Who is he?" I asked Manvika and Anamika, who were behind me.

"He is a professor. His name is Keith," Anamika replied.

"Oh! He's handsome. What happened to him? Why was he limping?" I asked.

"One of his legs is longer than the other. The right one is longer, I think," Anamika answered.

"Oh! How do you know?" I asked.

"One of my friends told me. He's good looking for sure," she said.

"Ya...he is." I smiled and we went for our class.

•

"Avantika! Can I use your internet?" Nisha asked, during the class.

"Ya sure!" I replied and gave her my cell phone. I had nothing to hide in my cell phone.

"My internet card has expired. So, I'll just check my Facebook account and give it back to you," she said.

I nodded.

After the class, she returned my phone saying that she was unable to check her account. Since it was the last class, we headed home after it was over. I reached home in another half an hour. After changing my clothes and having lunch, I opened Facebook on my mobile to check my account. As I opened the application, I saw six new messages in the message notification box. Thinking that it was my account as I usually don't log out before closing the application, I opened the message box. There were messages from people I didn't know. I was bewildered but suddenly remembered that Nisha had taken my phone. It was her account. I was about to log out when I saw Rohit's name in the message box. Unable to resist my curiosity, I opened his conversation with Nisha. I scrolled up to their first conversation. I was just curious to read how he had asked her for a movie.

The first conversation was initiated by Nisha herself and most of Rohit's replies were one-word answers with 'what about you?' written after them. The second conversation which took place after six days was also initiated by Nisha. I scrolled down but saw that he had never mentioned going out for a movie. I went back to the first conversation and read it. What I found out was simply unbelievable! I was disheartened to see the extent to which mere jealousy can lead a person to. Nisha had lied! Rohit had not asked her to meet him in college. He had just ended the mundane conversation with 'See you around in college' which Nisha exaggerated as 'he asked me to meet him in college today'. Whoa!

I read all the messages. He had not asked her for a movie! He had just said that he wanted to see a movie which was to be released in November but he was unsure of getting company as it was unpopular amongst boys. Further, he had added that he'd see it nevertheless with someone or the other because he was excited as it was the last part of the series. Wow!

So, I had never been committed to this guy, we weren't even the best of friends and one of my classmates and ex-friends, out of sheer jealousy and contemplating the possibility of our being together some time in the unforeseen future, had devised this 'evil master plan' to part us.

I was very angry with Nisha but I was also sad at the fact that even if Rohit didn't have any feelings for Nisha, he had not spoken to me in the past few days. In fact, he had even stopped greeting me in college. Perhaps, it was because he had waved to me in college one day while I was on the phone, which I hadn't noticed at that time. When I had realized that he had waved to me, I had turned around to reciprocate the gesture, but he had left by then.

I did not know who had sent the request to whom, but that did not matter now. Whatever the matter was, I made up my mind to always wave to him if I saw him in college and decided to break all my ties with Nisha. She was the real culprit.

Soul-Searching

After the realization of the truth, I should have been more interested in Rohit, but rather, I witnessed my interest in him diminishing to a minimal level. I was no longer interested in him, or any other guy for that matter. I was as disheartened as the knight who loses his favourite horse in the sands. Having searched and waited for his horse for days, neither he had the desire to accept some other, nor the strength to continue his search or to continue waiting. Being too tired of everything, I sought refuge in exploration.

I had applied for the post of a columnist in an independent newspaper of Delhi University in the beginning of August, but unfortunately, I had been late. The recruitment phase had already been over. I was now resorting to desperate measures to create a 'life' for me. I wrote to the HR Manager of three online magazines, mailed my CV and sample articles to them in order to get a job. But nobody really wanted a fresher to work for them. After all, they were online magazines with a good reputation! Well, not really. I had never even heard of them before. It was just that I was exploring my interests, which included writing. Well, they didn't reply to my emails. One did. But by that time, I was no longer interested.

I had started regarding everyone who had done some wrong to me in my 'about-to-be-18' years of life as 'blameless'. I did not blame the people who had been jealous of my lifestyle, looks or the fact that I always topped in my class; and those who instigated others against me, telling them things which I never knew I was supposed to have done until I heard them from others. Why? Because I thought that the world was like that. Almost everybody in this world can't bear to see the other person being better than him. In their attempts to raise their position a point above the others, people resort to bringing others down as against raising themselves up. If the people who did wrong to me are included in this bunch of insecure people and thus increasing their count, it won't matter because their count is already too high. Single drops won't affect the vast ocean anymore.

I did not blame Aarav for being a flirt, for not being true to one girl, for playing with my emotions and telling me that he loved me when he actually didn't, for breaking my heart and shattering it into pieces and for using me for his own selfish motives. Why? Because the world is like that. We use things which are immaterial to us. It is all about the word 'use' ultimately. The important point is whether the motives behind it are good or bad. It may be good from one person's perspective but bad from the other's. If Aarav was mean, it was his choice. If I wanted to change him to become a better person, then it was my problem. If I cannot forget him even after being aware of the reality, it will always be my problem, not his. After all, he cannot be blamed for who he is! Everything was messed up in my head.

Thinking so much about these things gave a new direction to my thought process. It was good that I had started forgiving people as it would help me to move on, but the worst part was that I had started blaming myself.

If it wouldn't have been Aarav, it would've been someone else. The problem is not with him. It is with me... my destiny. If it wouldn't have been Nisha, something or the other would've come between me and Rohit, because my destiny forbids me from experiencing happiness. Such were my thoughts now.

I abhorred going to college. I wanted to be alone. I was back to my childhood tricks where I would act unwell to shut myself in my room for the entire day, to not talk to anyone, but to listlessly stare at the ceiling, thinking about nothing. An occasional drop of tear would sometimes roll down my cheek, but I wouldn't cry. Sometimes I would set out for college, attend a few classes and come back. I would neither go to any new place to hang out when my friends would, nor would I sit in the cafeteria. I would act completely normal with my friends, poking fun at them, just to avoid unnecessary questions and let them feel that I was happy. My parents would give me medicines when I would take a leave from college and I would cleverly avoid taking them. I started making a zillion excuses, just to be alone.

At the time when I should've diverted my attention towards Rohit, I was lost... lost in the world of ghosts! Ghosts were my new interest. I would search for haunted places on the internet, watch scary videos and movies, read ghost stories and research on the paranormal world. I even liked the page 'Paranormal World Confessions' on Facebook and would spend hours having a glimpse of that world instead of focussing on the one I currently lived in! I was definitely lost.

I didn't want to expose Nisha publically because firstly, I wasn't sure about Rohit's feelings for me and secondly, I didn't want to let her know that I had checked her inbox and read her conversations with Rohit, to be honest. I had started ignoring her and we were no longer on talking terms.

When I could no longer rely on people, nature came to my rescue. I found a new routine to please me. The chirping birds, the green grass, lovely flowers, blossoming buds, falling leaves, butterflies and a garden chair became the key to relieve my disturbed mind. When I no longer wanted to attend college, I would head back home, stopping on the way to spend some alone time in the park which was few hundred metres from my home. I would tell my driver to go back home but I knew that he wouldn't. He would go to someplace to eat and return only after an hour, giving me enough time to return to my house, thus avoiding my mother's questions about where I was.

There was a half-elliptical gate from where one could see a canopy of flowers, without even stepping inside the garden, towards the left. Trees, plants and shrubs of every shape and size were surrounded by fences. A pigeon usually greeted everyone entering the garden with a 'hello' in its own different language. Beautiful butterflies would dance around the blossoming pink, white, yellow, red, purple and orange coloured flowers, characteristically behaving like asymptotes, getting closer and closer but never meeting each other. I would go and sit under my favourite umbrella-shaped shed above a cemented circular floor. I would observe everything happening around me very closely, noticing the intricacies of nature. People rarely visited the garden in the afternoon so I had peace and calmness around me.

I would sometimes smile as I would look at the birds playing hide and seek. A blissful sight it was, time and again. The pain engraved in my heart would find its antidote here as whenever I would visit the place, the pain would go away slightly. What Aarav was to me then, this place was to me now. I would sometimes take novels with me and they transported me into a different world and time without moving an inch and kept me engaged. I mostly read love stories or classics. I felt sad for the characters' sorrows and happy when they felt the same. Somewhere deep down, maybe I felt that the things which were done by men for their women in the books would, perhaps, never be done for me by someone I love. I gained an iota of hope when two lovers met after years of separation, in the books. A temporary refuge from reality… these paperbacks were. Whenever I completed a good book, I felt as if I had parted ways with a friend.

It was not as if I had only been exploring my interests or seeking some 'me-time' during this period. My life lay in chaos in front of me. I doubted the crucial decisions that I had made in my life, the ones which were entirely made by me and I regretted making them now. I was a Science student during my school days and had scored 97 percent in PCM in class 12th board exams, with an aggregate of 95.5 percent. As a school girl, Science was my duty, but literature was my desire. But now, I doubted my choice of giving my desire supremacy over my duty. I doubted opting for English Honours when I had the choice of choosing anything in the realm of Science. I cleared all the cut-offs of Science courses but didn't go for them. I wondered if a BA degree would do when I had the option of going for a BSc Degree. I regretted not taking up Maths Honours since I loved Maths too. I had taken the important decisions of my life following my heart. When I had listened to my heart, it said, "Go after your interest". When I had listened to people, they said, "You've scored such good marks, pursue something else".

I ignored the latter. But now I felt as if I had done injustice to the score I had obtained. My parents were very supportive and happy with whichever course I would have chosen. They didn't want to put any pressure on me. Everybody considered it an immature decision of brushing aside Engineering, Economics and other Science courses and opting for English Literature.

Relationship-wise, I had never showed much interest in anyone except Aarav, even though during high school there were many people asking me out. Maybe I could have had a better life if I had gone for someone other than Aarav, but I believed in my one true love, which was Aarav at that time. Now I wondered if it was always right to go for one's interests. Are our interests always meant to be held supreme? Was I right in following them? Would they earn me a better life? Or was I just being stupid in following my heart? I suddenly started feeling guilty for not choosing the Science courses and talked to my mother about that. I told her everything that was going on in my head regarding my course. I told her about the changes that I would come across after taking up literature, like marks, which were certainly not one of the positives of this course. She would say, "Nothing can be done now. Do well in whatever you've taken. The more you'll think about it, the more you'll get tensed."

How I wished to get rid of that guilt.

How I wished to go back in time and change my decisions.

How I wished to undo the decisions I had taken as far as relationships were concerned.

I was lost, like a boat without a bearing in the middle of the ocean. I needed to get out of this mess, sooner rather than later.

Freshers' Party

September had already begun. I looked at my life ahead with 'I-have-destroyed-all-my-future-happiness-and-prospects' attitude. Anyway, with the beginning of September, it was time for my department's freshers' party, to formally welcome the new students and create a platform for them to know the others associated with the department. I had already missed the informal one so I couldn't dare miss this one. The theme for the party was Harry-o-ween, a mixture of Harry Potter and Halloween. I was in college attending a class when the theme was announced by the seniors who made an effort of coming to our class on the third floor instead of just texting it to the class representative.

People were all chirpy and excited about the party. A change could be seen on that day. Students who were otherwise always found texting or playing games or checking their Facebook accounts during the class, were now heartily participating in the healthy group discussions based on 'how to dress for the party'. Our dear professors had shouted for us to calm down so much that I wondered if they would be able to speak the next day. Ultimately, the majority won and we were dismissed earlier than usual on that day; but that dismissal didn't come in the way of discussions. Anamika, Manvika and I headed towards home thinking that we would discuss it over WhatsApp after Googling. Ritvik loved to chat and put forward his views, so he stayed back. He wanted to be the 'popular guy' whom everybody greeted and listened to, a friend to everyone. Getting the title of the 'sexiest man alive' would have pleased him very much. I was a quiet person, always at peace, outwardly at least. I had never engaged in catfights since school and trust me, would have never even wanted to!

So, as planned, we Googled costumes. But, unfortunately, we found nothing substantial. I had my get-up in mind. I wanted to dress up like an evil person who performs black magic. All I needed was a black dress, a long black conical hat and long artificial nails which were supposed to be either black or red. Manvika and Anamika did not have anything in mind but both of them decided to wear a black dress.

Over the next weekend, I went shopping with my mother. We went to Lajpat Nagar Market.

"Mom. Come, come. Maybe we can find something in that showroom," I said with a rare optimistic attitude.

But surprise, surprise. We had gone through all the showrooms but hadn't found a single dress that would suit the theme. I didn't want a party dress, and those were all I could find. I didn't want it to be totally monstrous either. I was looking for something moderate.

All my hopes were lost as we headed back home from the market when suddenly my eyes caught a dress in a stall.

"Mom, mom! Wait! See that one," I called her.

I held the dress in my hand and found it to be perfect. So I got the dress for my freshers' party from the open market. Some alterations were made later. I already had the hat as I had once bought it for a school competition. I got the red nails from a nearby shop, and everything was finally in place.

The day arrived. I was dressed up in black, excited and looking forward to a great day. I had dressed to be remembered and not just to get noticed. I clicked some pictures before leaving the house, put my hat in a bag and left for college. I was very confident of my attire. It seemed good to me and my mother liked it as well. My father had left for work so he couldn't see me dressed for the party.

I was looking out of the window of my car when I thought I saw Aarav driving his car near Pragati Maidan. Although I couldn't be absolutely certain, I was pretty sure that it was him since I recognized his car, as Silver Nissan Micra. With this, my attention shifted back to him and the old days till I reached college. So much for letting go of the past!

I entered the college auditorium thinking that my friends would be there, but they weren't. There were some of my classmates though, and of course, seniors too. I called up my friends; they told me they were taking pictures outside and would come right in. They came after about ten minutes. Till then, I sat with my other classmates thinking that it would be rude to leave their company just like that.

"Wow! You look good," Anamika complimented.

"Nice!" Manvika said.

"Thanks! You guys look great too," I replied with a smile on my face.

I showed them my hat which they liked. They were dressed not too fancy like the others who were already in the hall.

Without my hat, I looked pretty normal too. I thought that it wouldn't be a good idea to wear it since everyone else hadn't really dressed up as per the theme and I put it back into my bag. In a few minutes, the event started. Ten minutes into the event, when I looked around, I could see magicians, ghosts, and witches all around. I figured out that it was time to wear my hat! I looked cute with that on, according to people.

We had an introduction round to begin with. Pizzas and cold drinks were served simultaneously. Since almost everyone was wearing black, and every girl was a witch when asked about her attire in the introduction round, I told the three judges that I was dressed up like an evil person who performs black magic rather than calling myself a witch. I was tired of hearing that word, and am sure everybody else was too! One of the judges said that he liked my get-up, especially my hat!

I just laughed and said, "Thanks!"

Twelve students out of the total sixty-six were shortlisted for the next round. Those who called themselves ghosts/witches but failed to convince the judges about being dressed like one and the defaulters who weren't dressed according to the theme were given the punishment of dancing on the stage in groups of three. They enjoyed themselves in that too, so it wasn't really a punishment. I was amongst the twelve shortlisted students while Ritvik, Manvika and Anamika ended up dancing in a group.

The next round was the talent round and we were asked to do anything we were good at. We were given ten minutes to prepare. We could dance in pairs too. Almost everyone chose to dance alone, except one pair. We were called in after ten minutes. I had decided to dance. After a few minutes, it was my turn.

"On which song would you like to dance?" asked the host.

"Well, let's not do it like this. We'll play a song and you'll have to dance to it," said one of the judges.

I nodded. A disco number was played, my kind of song. I danced and could see the audience applauding! They liked it and that gave me a lot of confidence.

"Okay. Now, we would like to see if you can dance to slow numbers," said another judge.

He continued, "Choose a partner for yourself."

I looked at the boys in the audience. I was about to choose a senior when they chose one for me, themselves. They chose the President of the Literary Club, Aditya, to be my partner and fortunately, we weren't complete strangers, being friends on Facebook.

"You are Avantika, right?" Aditya asked.

I responded, "Yup."

"Don't worry. They do this every year," he continued. I smiled as a romantic song was played. I don't know why but I could easily dance on that number. This was shocking because slow numbers weren't really my thing. Everyone was cheering for us and after dancing for about a minute, Aditya stopped and told the judges that it was enough. I had been dancing for three minutes though, because the male singer's line in the song came rather late. Everyone clapped and I was asked about my future goals by the judges. After answering their questions, I was asked to go join the spectators. Other participants also performed. There was dancing, singing, mimicry, taekwondo and stand-up comedy. Five people were shortlisted for the next round; I was one of them.

It was a rapid fire round where the participants had to say the first thing that came into their minds against a particular set of words.

"Love – Life
Future – Bleak
Clothes – Insufficient
College – Fun
Boyfriend – Hangouts…"

Such were my responses. I did manage to make everyone laugh at some of my responses.

Well, I wasn't crowned Miss Fresher but was crowned the Best Dressed. I wasn't particularly gunning for the crown; I just wanted this day to leave me with lots of good memories and that I had very well achieved. After taking close to two hundred pictures, my friends and I headed back home. I got a photograph taken with Aditya too. Shreya, one of my friends who lived nearby, was accompanying me in my car.

"You looked so good today. And you danced so well. Really well! Even Mayank was praising you," she said.

"Thanks! I had a great time," I replied. Mayank was one of our classmates.

From seeing Aarav to dancing with the President of the Literary Club and getting crowned, it seemed like a movie sequence, which climaxed when on our way back home, we had a flat tyre on the flyover and we had to pull over. It took around twenty minutes to do just that. Shreya and I had a nice chat during that time. It was 6.30 p.m. when I reached home after dropping her.

Upload the pics! It is eight o'clock! Upload. Them. Now! Texted Anamika.

All our pictures had been taken from my phone as it had a nice camera. It took me more than an hour to select and upload the pictures. Of course, the 'remove this photo' round followed after that. Eighty pictures made the final cut. I was so exhausted that I was logging out without even checking the notifications when a message popped up.

Hey!

It was Aditya. He already had a girlfriend and I had seen her cheering when we were dancing. She was pretty.

Hey. Sup? I replied.

Nothing much. You say?

Same. Was just uploading pics.

How did you like dancing with me?

It was good. You know, I was wondering about the same. Whether you liked dancing with me or not... I wrote.

I liked it. Why wouldn't I?? You were good. I don't really dance, you know.

LOL. No, you were good ☺

How did our pic turn out?

Wait, let me send it to you. I didn't find it good enough so I didn't upload it.

I said, feeling embarrassed on thinking that he must have felt bad about it.

Omg! I'm glad you didn't. I don't look good around pretty faces.

Nah..I have seen your photos with your girlfriend. They were rather good.

I added, *And that is just your modesty.*

He wrote, *No, no! Really! :P*

Okay! :P So I got to dance with the President today! :D

Haha :P This post really doesn't mean anything to me, you know :P Well, I just want to serve the people well. That's all :D he replied.

Oh I'm sure you're doing that very well. Well anyway, I'll catch you later. Very tired. It was a long day. Good night.:) I wrote.

Sure...Bye. Good Night☺

I fell off to sleep as soon as I lay down on the bed. I didn't even know who had turned off the lights when I woke up in the morning.

The Universe and Me

I don't know how and why but I had started enjoying college, and to such an extent that I didn't want to go back home after the classes were over. In a span of fifteen days, there wasn't a single eating joint that I had not set foot in. I would even miss classes and set out to give pleasure to my taste buds with Ritvik. From BTW to Chachake Chhole Bhature to Tom Uncle's Maggi to Spice Den, Big Boss, Shawarmawala, KFC, QD's, Barista, Chowringhee Lane, CCD, etc. We didn't leave out any food outlet! Food became my life.

Food, my newly found love, like the other love of my life, didn't bear with me. It affected my throat and I had to resort to medication after every two days. After fifteen days of extensive eating, it had developed a permanent tendency of getting choked and hurting even if I would just have a sandwich from the college cafeteria. It was as if my throat refused to take in anything except home-cooked food. I could even hear it saying, 'Don't even think of it' when I would come across Shawarmawala in Kamla Nagar, since that food outlet was my favourite. I would stay in college till late and till my stomach announced, 'I want good food. Go home.'

•

The DU elections were round the corner. Since the day I had entered college, I could see people campaigning for NSUI and ABVP giving away cards, pamphlets and making rounds in white SUVs inside the college premises. But, as the elections were approaching and since elections in Delhi University have a wide reach, I could see posters even in South Delhi. There were posters on the pole near my house! Candidates from college panels would come into the classes asking for votes and making hundreds of promises. On one such Tuesday, while I was bent over my book in class, around five to six candidates came inside. I was not listening to them and was busy reading. I didn't even see their faces. 'Mr. Darcy wrote a seven page letter to Miss Bennet…' was on my mind when suddenly I stopped reading. I had heard a name. Aarav Sharma. One of the candidates. It was as if I was struck by the God of Lightning himself. The world stood still when I heard that name.

I looked up.

Of course, he wasn't my Aarav but someone else with the same name. Talk about coincidences. Our class of all places. It had only been a few days since I had been thinking less about him and more about other things, but a mention of his name made all the memories come back crawling to the surface of my heart. Anyway, he was a guy from Physics Hons first year, and not too harsh on the eyes.

"Have you seen the condition of girls' common room? You were in power till this time and yet you did nothing to improve it!" said a daring girl of my class.

"We understand but it was being cleaned every day for the last two months, and every week its condition was checked by our people. Since we have now lost power and elections are going to be held again, we aren't working upon it," replied Aarav.

"We promise you that cleanliness will be one of our topmost priorities. The path near the stairs was filthy earlier. It was re-constructed by our people last year," a candidate said.

"We will work hard towards getting permission to introduce break time in the curriculum since you guys have long classes at a stretch," another candidate said.

They went on talking for I don't know how long, but I fell asleep while they were talking. Seeing everyone quiet, they felt that they had accomplished what they wanted, but well, what do they know!

While returning home, I made up my mind to introduce a thought filter in my mind which would filter out the thoughts of Aarav and only allow other meaningful thoughts to get in. I was focusing on the buildings and the traffic outside through the window of my car, when suddenly a car with AARAV written in big bold letters in red on its rear windshield passed by. What the hell! I felt like smashing my head on the window.

The next day when I entered college and was happily heading towards my class, I became a witness to an unimaginable sight! A boy who looked like Aarav was standing in the corridor. He could pass as Aarav's doppelganger. The same specs. Same height. Same hairstyle. Same sacred red thread on his right hand. Watch on the left. Same lips. Same manner of walking. Same voice even. But it wasn't him. Still, I was shocked! I took on the characteristics of a snail, walking as slowly as I possibly could. I soon found it to be humorous and made up my mind to tell Aarav about his doppelganger if we ever talked again!

Well, I had come to the conclusion that thoughts of Aarav could never be out of my mind because whenever it happened for two minutes at a stretch, something or the other would start haunting me with his memories. Take this doppelganger, for example. He would magically turn up in that very corridor at that very moment when I would come out of my classroom. It was as if the universe had conspired to not let us meet but not allowing us to forget each other either. How I wished that he'd face these kinds of encounters and meet a girl named Avantika to remind him of me. How I wished him to miss me! I wished my shadow to be cast in his life like his was being cast in mine. I wanted us to meet at a heavenly place guided by these shadows. Were all these things a symbol of the fact that we were made for each other? If not, then could everything be termed as a coincidence? Every damn thing? I didn't even know when it would stop, if it does, that is!

But what was troubling me more was that I wasn't even sure what I wanted anymore.

Keith Sir

It was the first time that I was wearing a kurti with leggings in college, a welcome change from jeans and top, which was my usual attire. A woman in black with my hair clipped with a clutch, I was feeling different that day.

"OMG! You look so beautiful," Kanika, a classmate, complimented.

"Wow! I like your kurti. You are looking gorgeous," Aastha seconded.

I had always felt some sort of connection with Aastha, perhaps maybe because she was from a Science background too.

"Avantika, looking good!" said Anamika and Manvika simultaneously.

To all the compliments, I replied with a "thanks" and a polite smile.

When Ritvik saw me, he kept looking at me without saying anything. He just stood staring at me, quiet, with eyes wide open as if he had seen something unbelievable. Embarrassed as I was on his reaction, I headed for the class without even greeting him. Jeez!

"Avantika! Stop! Stop!" shouted Anamika at the top of her voice.

I was about to open the door of the classroom when she stopped me. I stopped suddenly, standing motionless with no implicit response to Anamika's voice. I could see a tall man inside the classroom, a professor who was teaching his students but at that moment was looking towards the door at me. He was the same professor whom I had encountered in the staircase, the one who limped while walking. Embarrassed again, I quickly moved away from the door and went to Anamika who was sitting on the seating wall in front of that classroom as the next class was ours. Everyone burst out laughing. I could see the people inside the class looking at me. I blushed a beetroot red.

"Hey! I thought you were a teacher when I saw you from a distance," said Karan, one of my classmates who had recently arrived on the scene.

I just smiled.

More classmates came, smiled, greeted each other and soon everyone was talking to each other. It was quite natural for the class which was going on inside the room to get disturbed. We were no longer sincere students, but rather a group of chattering birds. I was always the silent one though, and this time was no exception. I had been removed from my original place beside Anamika and was now on the periphery of the big circle full of students making incessant noise. No sooner did my eyes fall on the tall professor than he gestured to me by folding his hands and moving both his hands to the right hand side, indicating that we should move from that place and go somewhere else to chatter!

I was not the culprit in this case and was quiet like a swan at peace. I was the one who had been asked to 'command' everyone to move away from the classroom. As if I could scream louder than them! But I, somehow, managed to tell them that sir was 'requesting' us to go away and within a couple of minutes, the place was empty. I found his polite way of telling us to leave quite contrary to what is expected of a professor. But it was really sweet of him to do so instead of coming outside and shouting at us!

"He is very sweet. He folded his hands and gestured to me to go away instead of shouting!" I said.

"Who? Keith sir?" Anamika asked.

"Oh yes! I had forgotten his name. What's his full name?" I asked.

"Keith Joseph," she replied.

"And yes, he is a good person. Some people even think that he is a flirt because of his polite ways!" she confirmed.

I nodded.

The class got over in five minutes and we were standing in front of a vacant classroom when I saw our seniors moving out. I was looking at them when Keith sir happened to pass by. He was wearing a brown kurta and blue jeans. He looked handsome.

"Thank you," he said, smiling. He even bowed his head!

Before I could register what he had said, he was gone with some students following him.

"You know what! Keith sir said 'thank you' to me. Can you believe that? He even bowed his head. How can a professor be so polite? And thanks? For what? I didn't do him a favour. In fact, it was his right to teach without any disturbance." I said, facing Anamika.

"Yes, he is very polite." she replied.

"And I saw our seniors coming out from the classroom. He teaches English?" I asked.

"Yes. He will teach us next year, maybe," she replied.

With this conversation going on, we reached our classroom. I was amazed at Keith sir's politeness and sweetness.

Birthday

September was about to end, which meant that my birthday was approaching. The fifth of October was the date. Everyone was excited except me. My friends were on the verge of getting a lavish treat and family was delighted to see me turn eighteen. My birthdays usually consisted of a small party with a few friends, gifts and celebrations over dinner with my family. Gifts were the best part though! I wanted to celebrate my eighteenth birthday with Aarav and I had been making plans for this day for the past year. But plans, excitement, happiness, hope... everything ended when we broke up. But there was still an iota of hope that he would wish me and that kept me going. Well, maybe not an iota of hope! I was a cent percent sure that he would wish me and had even framed the conversation that we would then have, in my mind. I had made it a point to convince him to come for my birthday party or at least meet me so that I could spend the day or a part of it with him. So that meant that I was waiting for my birthday more than anyone else because that was the only day which brought with itself a possibility of getting in touch with Aarav.

It seemed as if I was the first one to turn up for class. I could see nobody around Room No. 28, where our class was to take place. Keith sir was taking a lecture in that room. Sitting on the seating wall in front of that room, I texted Anamika to check whether we had a class. I received a positive response. Having nothing else to do, I began observing Keith sir. His reflexes, handwriting, way of speaking, teaching skills, nothing escaped my eyes. I utilized every second of the five minutes that I had, before our class began. I think I had a crush on him, and it began from the moment he had been 'polite'. He had a British accent and a nice handwriting. Spoke well. Moved his hands rhythmically with the flow of his speech while explaining something. He seemed to be a good teacher. I would greet him a good morning or afternoon whenever he happened to pass by.

"Hey!"said Anamika, who had just arrived.

"Hi!" I said back.

She asked, "Sup?" having nothing better to say.

"Nothing," I replied, having nothing better to say.

Soon, more students started arriving.

Seeing that the students had started coming out of the room, one of my classmates took me inside, pulling my hand. I was behind her so I was out of the view as she was tall and bulky. I saw Keith sir sitting on the teacher's desk and listening to a blind girl. He was quite focussed till he saw my classmate.

"What?"he asked. She was standing next to the desk, and looking at him, waiting for him to leave.

"We have a class here," she said.

"I haven't left till now. I am still here," he said, quite unlike the way he had spoken to me before. No smile. No politeness.

Just the rude 'I-am-a-professor-respect-my-presence' type of reply.

I was shocked to see that. A sudden transition? Or was he really like that? Whatever!

I was glad that he had not seen me as I vanished as soon as the words came out of his mouth, like I had just been told that my plane leaves in two minutes while I was still at the ticket counter. Somehow I wanted to be in his good books, I wasn't sure why. Well, anyhow, we went inside the classroom some time later.

My professor was busy explaining the theories given by Darwin and Marx, while I was busy scrolling down my WhatsApp contact list for any new status updates.

Tarika : 'Bored in class. Wanna sing. Lalala!'

Kashish : 'Your arms are my castle… your heart is my sky.'

I was used to not going through the contacts list in any particular order. I looked at people's status updates randomly.

Aarav : 'In love… <3<3'

What?? When?? How?? Why??

I was taken aback. Completely shaken!

Really?? Who.Is.That.Witch??

I could feel my throat becoming heavy, my eyes becoming watery, my heartbeats becoming faster, my senses becoming numb and the detective inside me coming to the forefront!

From Facebook to Viber, I visited all his profiles and researched for the next two hours, thoroughly! I was not at all bothered about being thrown out of the class or being called by my friends. I was lost.

After two hours, I finally got the answer when he updated his status to 'I love you, Kriti' and put her profile picture in place of his. Meanwhile, I had completely lost awareness of the surroundings. My friends had been asking me so many questions, but I was oblivious of their presence. But I didn't care about that. I was too overwhelmed by emotions and after being repeatedly asked what was wrong, I surrendered to my emotions and had a good cry in front of my friends.

"Don't worry. We'll find a better guy for you," said Avantika, tapping my shoulder.

"I love him," I said with an emotionally heavy voice.

"I'm in love with my ex too," she said.

"But your love is different than mine," I said.

She didn't say anything. Neither did Manvika. Nor did I.

I headed for home without attending the rest of the classes and they didn't stop me. Perhaps, they knew that I wouldn't.

Was I not worth it? Was the power of my love so weak that I could not get him back? Was it so easy for him to move on, so quickly?

And a million questions like these started wandering in my mind. I was shattered…again. I already knew that he wasn't mine, but his being single gave me a sense of relief. It was over now. All over!

I had been planning to spend my birthday with him. I guess I had received my birthday present too early! Maybe she'll treat him badly and he'll then realise my importance. Stupid childish hopes!

I no longer wanted to associate myself with any activity. I wanted to be locked in my room, have my meals there, spend some quality 'me' time and be cut off from the rest of the world. If not this, running away to a place far far away from where I was – a remote island maybe, where people didn't speak my language, a place where I knew nobody – would have been great. Usually people get attuned to pain when they experience it in abundance, but this time again, I couldn't handle it. The realisation that he did not love me, even though I knew that already, was too painful to bear. Simply not having the courage to get out of my house and face the world, put on a fake smile and not allow my tears to flow, I missed college for a week, giving my parents the false excuse of the department trip that I didn't want to go on. I would come out in front of my family members rarely, had interest in nothing and followed the mundane pattern of eating, sleeping and stalking. I had told everyone that I was going on a holiday with my family so that my friends would not pester me. Sometimes I felt like replying, "I'm in hell! Wanna join me?" if anybody did pester me.

Days passed. Two days were left for the much-awaited occasion of my eighteenth birthday. This birthday was much needed because this day was the only hope of getting to talk to Aarav. I was sure that he would wish me. He didn't love me but we had been together for two years. Two damn years! And he had no right to forget me like that. As it was my eighteenth birthday and it comes once in a lifetime, I had no intention of spoiling it. Being incapable of spending it at home, I called up my school friends to remind them that my birthday was round the corner, which unexpectedly, they did remember. Kanika, my best friend during school, was the first one I called.

"Hey," I said when she picked up the phone.

"Bitch! Where are you lost? No phone calls, no messages. Have you managed to find a guy for yourself or what?" she burst out.

"No, it's not like that. I was a little busy. Well, my birthday is…" I had not even completed when she interrupted.

"I know! Did you think that I will forget your birthday? My sister's birthday? We're having a party at GK. Inviting people is your job. Timings are 12-7.00 p.m Now tell me what's going on in your life?" she declared and asked.

"Wow! Pretty fast. Nothing much. I am single. Aarav got someone new and..." I said.

"Got it. You need a new boyfriend, Avantika. Why don't you look out for someone new?" she asked, again.

"You know about the whole Rohit incident, don't you? I tried to put Aarav behind me and you know how it ended," I replied.

"It was not your fault, girl! Misunderstandings were created between the two of you. The world doesn't consist of two boys. There is a huge bunch of hot boys out there," she said.

"Haha! I know, baby. Umm... Did you manage to find a guy?" I asked.

"No. But I will. We both will," she said.

"Yeah. I love you!"

"I love you too, sista," she reciprocated.

"I gotta call some people now. Catch you on WhatsApp. See ya," I ended the conversation.

"See ya," she said and we hung up.

Then began the job of inviting friends. Most of them were uncertain about coming.

I went to college the next day as I couldn't afford to miss any more classes. Missing even two days at a stretch made a lot of difference and I already knew that I would have missed a lot during the last seven days. I was excited about the day after. I could feel the adrenaline rush. I wanted the clock to miss the coming hours and strike twelve, for I could see a light at the end of the tunnel. A part of me didn't want the time to pass and the next day to arrive because shattered hopes would be highly unbearable. But the hopeful part undermined the former one. Well, about my plans for my eighteenth, I had decided that I would go to college in the morning to treat my college friends and then leave at twelve to join my school friends at the decided venue.

By evening, everybody had confirmed that they would be coming except Rakesh, who had a presentation in college. Three boys and four girls were to be a part of it, including Rakesh. When I came back home from college, it was 2.30 p.m. and by the time, I received confirmations, it was 6.30 p.m. I had gone to get myself a birthday dress in the meantime.

"Happy Birthday, sweetheart! We'll make your day memorable tomorrow, I promise," Kanika was the first one to call. It was 12.05 a.m.

"Thank you so much," I replied.

"What are you wearing tomorrow?" she asked.

"Not tomorrow, today!" I said, laughing.

"Oh ya...today," she said laughing.

"A blue dress," I said.

"Yay! It would look great on you. You're gonna look hot!" she predicted.

"Hey! I'm getting a call. Talk to you later," I lied.

"Okay. Bye. Happy Birthday once again," she said excitedly and hung up.

Happy Birthday. God bless you. Love you...<3 read Gunjan's message.

Happy Birthday baby, muah read Diksha's message.

More messages followed, but not the one I craved for.

I couldn't sleep. The clock struck one. Aarav had not wished me. It was way too depressing for me. I felt like cancelling every plan. I really had not expected that.

I woke up in the morning, told myself that the day had to still go on and dragged myself to get ready. When I was changing my earrings, my cell phone rang. It was nine in the morning. I ran but it was an unknown number so it I thought that it couldn't be Aarav. Hopelessly, I picked it up.

"Hello."

It was Aarav.

Avowal

I did not have to hear his voice twice to know that it was him. I remembered his voice as clear as a crystal. I knew my hopes wouldn't betray me this time. I knew he would call me. I knew he couldn't be this cruel to me, for I was his Avni.

"Aarav…" I whispered.

I could feel the lump in my throat. I could feel the tears pooling in my eyes. I knew that I would start crying if I said one more word.

"Happy Birthday, Avni," he wished me.

Avni. Hearing that name gave me goose bumps.

"Thank you so much, Aarav," I said sobbing.

I tried to, but could not stop my tears from flowing.

"Avni, are you crying? I know you are. What happened?" his voice was full of concern for me.

"I love you, Aarav." I gave up. My feelings won over my rational self.

"Avni, I am sorry. I know that whatever I did to you was wrong and even if I apologise a thousand times, I can't heal your wounds."

I interrupted while he was saying this.

"Aarav, please don't," I said.

"Listen to me, Avni. Let me speak and please don't say anything in between. What I'm going to say now, I've never ever said that to anyone because nobody is as special as you are," he said.

"Avantika, you are the best girl I've come across in my life till now. I know I won't find another like you. I know that your love is magnificent and beautiful. I know people will think I'm crazy if I don't date a girl like you. But I'm sorry Avni, I can't play with your feelings. I cannot lie to you. I can't hurt you. I am not made for love. I am incapable of love. I can't love anyone. Not even you. I can't be with you because I don't deserve you. I am not a good person. You think that I am, but I'm not. You'll get a better guy. In fact, you deserve the best. It is not your fault that I don't love you. You have everything – beauty, money, talent, intelligence, a kind heart, a decent character. You are a good soul. There's nothing that is missing in you. The only problem is the way I am. I am the problem. I am not a good person," he continued.

Tears kept rolling down my cheeks as he said this.

"But you love Kriti, right? That means you are capable of love. Please don't lie," I said.

"I don't," he replied.

He continued, "I don't love her, but she's my girlfriend."

I said, "She can be your girlfriend when you don't love her, then why not me?"

I knew I was being stupid, but that was for later.

"Because you're different from all the other girls. I don't want to give you the false notion that I love you when I actually don't. You deserve better than this, Avni," he said.

"Promise me that you'll date a guy, move on and forget me. I have given you only pain and nothing else. Live for yourself, Avni. Hate me if you can, but please don't spoil your life because of me. You can do anything, achieve great heights and I'll be your friend forever. I'll be with you Avni, but as a friend."

"But I can't forget you, Aarav. I've tried. I love you. I can't live without thinking about you. How can you expect me to be happy without you when you are my only source of happiness? Where can I go when you're the only destination I know? How can I be satisfied without you when you are the only thing I crave for?" I burst out crying.

"Avni... please don't do this to yourself. There is nothing you can't do. You don't have to live without me. I'll be there as your friend. Trust me, Avni. I don't deserve you," he said.

"People can't remain friends for a lifetime," I said.

"That's all I can give you," he said.

"Aarav, can I ask for something?"

"Yes," he replied.

"I've always wanted to spend my eighteenth birthday with you. Can you please come to my birthday party today? It's in GK."

"Sorry I can't join you for the party. I've some work."

"Please just one day," I pleaded.

"I don't like saying no to you. I am sorry but I can't," he said.

"Okay," I said.

"Listen, I'll talk to you later. I have to go. Enjoy your day," and he hung up.

"Bye," I said.

There was a certain sense of obscurity when it came to his behaviour. His decision to leave had always been so sudden, be it phone calls or someone's life!

Manvika, Anamika and Ritvik were the first ones I gave my birthday treat to, before I met my school friends. Manvika and Anamika had given me a white dress and a card. Ritvik brought chocolates – loads of them. I got warm hugs and lots of birthday wishes from my classmates. It felt good.

I met my other buddies in GK. Rakesh was supposed to come after six so the party was still incomplete. We went to a pub and danced till our stomachs forced us to stop. Demanding food, they led us to a restaurant where we ordered North Indian and Chinese food. It was four o'clock then. Since we felt that the food was taking an unusually long time to arrive, I decided to take a look at the gifts. Flowers, chocolates, cards, dresses and accessories – basically everything a girl wants was what I had received. We ate like a group of nomads who had not eaten since days when the food arrived. Since we were a group of non-hookah lovers and non-alcoholics, fruit beer was the beverage of our choice. Well the only thing missing in the party was a big chocolate truffle cake which arrived with Rakesh, who surprised me by coming early. He came an hour before the expected time. He had brought flowers. The whole place looked like a garden now with so many flowers around. I giggled thinking that my bed would literally become a bed of roses. And I would lie upon it like a princess.

The last part of the day concluded with a lavish dinner with family which was preceded by another cake cutting ceremony. I felt as if I had put on two kilograms on that day.

One thing would always hurt me deep down, I thought as I was lying down on my bed. Although Aarav did realise the extent of my love for him, knew that he had hurt me and felt sorry for the same, he did not make an effort to fulfil my wish of many years by being with me on my birthday. He didn't even care to meet me. I was not hurt because he did not fulfil my wish, but rather because he knew that it would hurt me and still said 'no'.

When Life Took a Turn

The birthday week was over. And I was back to attending classes full time.

So, here I was, in college before time as usual. Sitting outside the classroom, eagerly waiting for a familiar face to show up. My favourite teacher had met with an accident the day before. Our CR had informed us on our WhatsApp group about the same.

A new professor was ready to fill in her place. Every single person whom I like was to eventually leave me. My stars didn't even spare my favourite teacher. I thought I shouldn't even dream of liking an individual because he would be snatched away from me later on. Was this the bitter truth of my life? Living all alone?

Nobody had come when I saw Keith sir entering our classroom.

Whoa! Was he our new teacher? Seriously? Where are the others? So many questions started popping up in my head.

I went inside, mustering all the courage I had gathered in the last eighteen years of my life.

"Good morning, sir," I greeted him.

"Good morning," he said.

"I'm the replacement for Niharika ma'am. Where are the others? Is today a mass bunk?"he asked.

"No, sir. They must be coming," I replied.

"Oh! I am early," he said, looking at his watch.

"Anyway, sit. What all have you people done till now?"

I answered, "We're through with more than half the book."

"That is good. So, I don't have much to complete. But the last portion of the book is really important. I hope I won't need extra classes since we still have a month to go for exams," he said.

"May I come in, sir?" asked a classmate.

More people followed. Soon people came in like swarm of flies.

Do I need to mention that I giggled all through his class? The answer is an obvious yes. I kept admiring his accent. He spoke each word laying emphasis upon it so that his words were clear despite his speaking fast. The girls found him hot but his limping didn't go well with them.

"CRs, let's exchange numbers now," Keith sir addressed the CRs after the class.

I did not pay attention to what he taught in class as I was busy paying attention to his accent and being teased by my friends. I obviously heard his words, but didn't register them in my mind.

"Avantika... Lucky girl! Your crush is here! I know you want to be the CR now. Eh?" Manvika teased.

I said, "I would love to be, you know. But then, who says admiring from a distance isn't fun?" And we all burst out laughing.

●

Life can get pretty weird when you dress to impress a teacher rather than young boys around you. Or, when suddenly, a desire emerges to get a new hairstyle. Or, when after fifteen days of declaration of results, you sit and ponder over it. Or, when you decide to drop every desire of your newly-changed self and on returning to your old self, you find a distraction coming in your way out of nowhere that gives your life a new turn.

Keith sir had been teaching us for fifteen days now. It's not that I had been thinking about him 24X7, but somehow, I happened to make an extra effort to look good on the days he'd take classes. I knew that many teens have crushes on their teachers, but on examining my recent behaviour, I wondered if it was normal. I tried to reason the efforts I was making and I felt like the most stupid person ever born. I thanked the faculties of my mind for arousing me from my deep imaginative slumber and casting some light on the reality I was living in.

Welcoming the sixteenth day, I dressed myself in the plainest clothes I had ever worn. Looking forward to making some good notes which would help me in my exams, I reached college. The first was Keith sir's lecture and I was not excited. I really wasn't.

"Is your class interested in attending lectures or not? Do you want me to wrap up without explaining anything? Why didn't you people turn up for the extra class yesterday?"

He seemed angry. Very angry.

Oh wait! What? Extra class? When?

"Sir, we didn't know about the extra class," said somebody when I was thinking about all these questions.

"You didn't know? I had conveyed the message to the CR of your class that I would be meeting you people at 2.15 p.m.

Fifteen students in total were present. Where were the rest of you? Kamla Nagar Market?" he taunted.

"But nobody told us about the class, sir," a really studious bunch of students complained. I could feel the terror in their voices at the thought of having missed important points.

"How many students did not know about the class?" Mr Joseph asked.

In reply, more than half of the class raised their hands.

"CRs, is it not your responsibility to forward the message to each and every individual of your class?" he said angrily.

I was like, okay…slow down, Mr Joseph. It was just a class!

"Sir, I didn't have balance in my phone so I could not call or text the students. I conveyed the message to those whom I saw and asked them to tell others too," one of the CRs said.

This CR was not on WhatsApp. None of the others to whom the message was conveyed, bothered to post it on our class chat group.

"Were there no classes yesterday?" he enquired.

The infuriated studious group replied, "Yes, there were."

Mr Joseph asked the CR, "Why was the announcement not made during the classes?"

The CR said, "I made the announcement sir, but nobody listened."

Liar! Liar! Pants on fire!

"No sir, he didn't," a boy who disliked the CR spoke.

Mr Joseph asked, "Where's the other CR?"

"She's absent."

"Was she absent yesterday?" Mr Detective asked.

"No, sir." LOL!

"What kind of a class is this? I want to complete my syllabus in the next ten days. I want someone who is regular and responsible to take over the responsibility of being the CR of my class."

Quietness had engulfed the class. I noticed his features very minutely at that time. He had a well-structured nose, big eyes, his teeth were symmetrical and lips weren't too big or small. His hair was thick and a little curled from above. He had the perfect jaw line. A little beard suited him.

"Avantika Sareen! Why don't you take up this responsibility?" he asked. It seemed more like a command than a question. I was befuddled for a few seconds there. A lot of mixed emotions too. So he thought that I was a good student? Hmm...interesting. But, it was a hectic job. But then only ten days!

I replied in the affirmative.

"Good, so as I will be teaching you in the next semester also, Avantika remains the CR of my class till the end of the next semester," he announced.

Not ten days? Okay!

Confession time! It was not that I was happy about my favourite teacher meeting with an accident. I missed her still. But I didn't mind Keith sir teaching us either.

Keith sir instructed, "Avantika, write your email and contact number on a piece of paper and hand it over to me."

"And take down my number," he dictated his number.

I handed over the piece of paper to him and the class continued as usual.

"CR? Eh?" With this, my friends started pulling my leg till the time my stomach began to hurt with the laughing. That is what friends are for, I guess!

Exams

When I saved Keith sir's number on my phone, I had not thought of it as a golden chance to stalk him. On checking WhatsApp, while going down the list of contacts, I found a new name waiting for my eyes to hang on to. It was Keith sir's. That meant that I could keep an eye on him, but he could keep a track of my status updates and DPs too if he had the habit of going through everyone's updates. Whatever I wrote had to be filtered three times now. First for Aarav. Second for professors. Third for general public.

Sound of a bird humming. A WhatsApp message from Anamika. A Facebook link.

After logging in, I was surprised. Whoa! Bwahaha!

Keith sir's profile appeared on my phone. I went through his profile before replying to her. Gosh! He was popular! He had many students as his friends. Some really hot pictures. Weird football lovers' statuses. Mark Zuckerberg as one his subscriptions. Eighteen subscribers. Worked at Hindu College.

The rest was not public. In one of the pictures, he was with a really short girl and that reminded me of the characters in *Gulliver's Travels*. Nerd Alert!

Also, I saw one of his pictures in which he was wearing aviators and was surrounded by ice. It was Kashmir or so said the comments. He should try modelling, I thought.

Staring at his pictures? pinged Anamika.

No. At his wife's pictures, I joked.

Wife? Send me a screenshot. I didn't see that. He's married? I never knew that.

I replied, *Yes, he's married. Go online. See for yourself.*

Send me the screenshot, na! I'll have to open it again, replied the lazy ass.

I replied, *I've logged out.*

Okay:(.

She pinged after five minutes, *Where is it?*

What? I was laughing.

That pic which you were talking about. I couldn't find it.

I thought of fooling around with her some more.

Check in mobile uploads.

I did. It wasn't there.

Check again, lazy ass.

It is not there. Liar!

Hahaha…I was kidding.

Bitch! As expected.

•

Lately, I had developed an interest in doing other things rather than stalking people. Yes, I no longer stalked my ex. Stalking Keith sir was a farfetched idea. Doing other things included working out, reading and studying. The last one was more like a compulsion than an option and was replaced by watching movies most of the time.

Avantika, I've mailed you a couple of critical essays. Please forward them to others. See you – Keith Joseph

This was the message left by Mr Joseph later on the day when we exchanged flowers…err…numbers, I meant. The chat app played a part in this message. I like the time when pigeons were used. So romantic! Anyway, coming back to the point, this was my first WhatsApp message from a professor.

Sure, sir. See you. I replied.

After replying, I began taking a look at people's status updates. One read as 'Angoor Aadmi.'

'Who's this maniac?' I thought. I burst out laughing the next second. It was Keith sir!

"I want to shake hands with penguins," I told Ritvik about this fantasy of mine. The change in his expressions made me laugh. He was first straight faced, then made a weird face conveying disgust I suppose, a round of laughter followed afterwards.

"Why? Why would you do that?" he asked, while laughing.

"Because I want to," I said.

"They are slippery. Not even cute," he started pronouncing judgments on the poor creatures.

I could have taken the conversation further but Keith sir had entered the room. He had put forward an argument for discussion. He wanted to wind up his syllabus in five days instead of ten as he would be busy in the first week of November. Our class had decided to take preparatory leave from 7 November, dismissing the announcement of the actual leaves from 11 November. Our exams were starting from 18 November and ending on 28 November. Everybody agreed to come for his extra classes and all was well in the world.

Days passed. Exams approached. I had been underlining the important parts of the texts all these days. I went anti-social with only my books for company.

On the day of my first exam, on seeing the number of students around the notice board, I had no hope of figuring out my room number. But then, a friend came and told me my room number. Phew! The paper was easy. The first exam went well. Summing up the entire ten days that followed afterwards, the first and the last exam went well. Period. Those in between shouldn't be talked about.

It was the day of my last exam. I wanted to have fun, explore a new place, eat and party. But, I had forgotten one simple rule of my life: Whatever I wanted, would not be given to me, except the want of studying literature which I was currently pursuing. After the exam, I sat for about one-and-a-half hours with Ritvik, talking about all sorts of things – from marriage to planets. But after forty-five minutes, we were in the midst of a debate. The next half an hour or so was spent in the fruitful exercise of debating. Anamika had a birthday party to attend. Manvika had to help her friend in doing. I don't know what, and Ritvik had to write an exam for a visually impaired candidate, so there was to be no party. As soon as Ritvik left for Hans Raj College, I left for home. On the way to the college's gate, I encountered Mr Joseph. He smiled at me. I reciprocated.

"How was your exam?" he asked.

"Good, sir," I replied.

And we went our respective ways.

●

I had a month before college would start again. But, sleeping till late was still an unrealised hope. I had several goals to be accomplished during that one month. I wanted to join a gym to tone my body and this was primarily the reason why I couldn't afford to sleep till late. I found morning workouts easier than the evening ones. My driving classes were ready to take off from December. It was a fifteen-day exercise, but the latter half of the month was to be spent practising on congested roads, expressways, toll roads and so on. My father had promised me that my driving licence would be ready before college re-opened, and then I could drive to college. I had a list of books to read and movies to watch. In short, I was going to be busy. I had not made any plan to go out of Delhi with my family because I hated missing out on the Delhi winters. This time around, I didn't seem to have any time too.

Exposure

Holidays had begun a few days back. My daily routine consisted of waking up at 6.00 a.m., hitting the gym at 7.00 a.m., coming back home at around 8.30 a.m. which was followed by bathing and eating. I would leave for my driving lessons at 10.00 a.m., return at 11.15 a.m., doze off to sleep till 2.00 p.m. and have lunch at 2.00 p.m. while watching TV. I would roam around in the house doing nothing and have long gossip sessions with my mother. Her suggestions to lose weight and improve my driving, random conversations and Facebook gave me company till 4:00 p.m. Reading books or watching movies would keep me engaged till 7.00 p.m. I'd have an early dinner then, as per my gym instructor's recommendation. Watching TV, chatting with friends and reading would mark the end of the day. This routine was occasionally disrupted when I had to go out for some reason or the other.

I would feel lonely at times, brooding over my past, present and future but could hardly change anything. The pain of loneliness is registered in the same part of the brain as physical pain. That would explain what I would feel sometimes. I knew that I had friends but they were not true, at least that's the vibe I used to get. Nobody would help me if I were to be caught in a major crisis, I thought.

I was catching up with my friends at Starbucks in CP one day. As soon as I entered, I saw someone getting up from his seat with his friends. It was not Aarav.

"Hello, sir." I greeted Mr Joseph as he crossed my path.

"Hello, Avantika."

I won't lie. I did find his voice kind of sexy.

"Enjoying your freedom?" he asked and smiled at me.

I laughed.

"Yes, sir," I replied.

He said, "I'm here with a friend. Teachers enjoy freedom too."

I replied, "I can understand, sir".

"See you next month," he said with a smile.

It was 18 December. I checked my Yahoo! Mail. It had been a month since I had done so. I had 257 new mails. All of them from stupid sites I had subscribed to, except one. It was from the HR of the independent newspaper of Delhi University, *DU Times*, for which I had applied. I had been shortlisted and an interview was to confirm my selection. The HR manager had given her number and asked me to call, since I had not provided my number in the CV. I hadn't? Must've forgotten. I had received the mail a week ago. I rushed to get my phone. and dialled the number. Nobody picked up. I panicked. What if my place belonged to someone else now? What if I'm late? What if they don't need more people? Crap!

I left a message on the number which was given in the mail.

Hello! I had received a mail informing me that I have been shortlisted for the editorial team of DU Times. I am sorry to respond late. Had not checked my mail for a while. Text me when I can call you. – Avantika Sareen.

After four hours of endless waiting, my phone rang.

Shruti, HR Manager, was flashing on the screen.

I picked up. "Hello."

"Hello, Avantika. I'm Shruti, the HR Manager of *DU Times*."

"Hi! I'm sorry. I saw your mail today only," I said.

"It's okay. Don't worry about that," she said.

"So, I'm going to ask a few questions. Okay?" she asked.

"Ya, sure," I said.

I was nervous. This was my first job interview. Not that I was going to be paid for working. It was more for self-satisfaction. It was the newspaper of Delhi University, after all! All my friends longed to get in. Many had applied and I had been shortlisted. I had left Science to achieve something in the field of writing. I didn't want to lose this opportunity.

"So, why should we take you?" the first question that she asked.

"I can write about any topic and that too, a good piece. The intensity of my dedication towards writing made me grab the opportunities of writing articles for national newspapers like the *Hindustan Times* as part of school initiatives. I'll do my work with utmost sincerity and complete it before time. You must have already read about my qualifications and experiences in the CV. I don't need to elaborate on that. I can surely prove to be an asset to your newspaper," I answered, flawlessly.

"Okay. So what do you write about?" was the second question.

I answered, "Everything from poetry to articles on political or social issues."

"Okay. So, Avantika, you were already selected on the basis of your sample writings and CV. These questions were asked more as a part of getting to know you than as part of the selection process. Welcome to the *DU Times* team."

I was selected. And naturally, I was ecstatic.

"Thank you," I replied.

"We have meetings every Tuesday in which we discuss about the topics we're gonna write about and other important issues. They are held at 3.30 p.m. at Max Mueller Bhawan, CP and it is mandatory to be present in the meetings. As you are new, you'll be marked on the basis of your work and attendance in the meetings for the first three months, after which you'll be permanent. Will you be able to come for the meetings?" Shruti asked.

I replied, "Yes."

"Great! More information will be given to you on 20 December, the day after tomorrow. You have to attend a meeting along with the other new interns at Max Mueller Bhawan. Will you be there?" she asked.

I answered, "Yes, I'll be there."

She said, "Okay. The editor will brief you about the rest of the things. Be there at 12.00 p.m. sharp."

I said, "Yes, sure."

She added, "Alright. All the best. Work hard. We have parties too. Don't think that it's all work and no play for you. Hope you have a great time with us."

I replied, "I hope the same."

It was the day of my first meeting. I was asked to reach the venue by noon, but I was fifteen minutes early. I had no idea how the other team members looked in reality. Since I had also been added to the DUT group on WhatsApp, I only knew them through their DPs. I kept looking in all directions, searching for a face I could recognize but all my efforts were futile. I called Shruti. She asked me to go to the cafeteria area and look for a huge bunch of chattering people! I did the same but encountered many such groups. I checked the faces in the DPs once more. None of them matched with those around. Twenty minutes passed. I was standing there like an idiot, looking for people I had never seen before and most of whom were making weird faces in their profile pictures. Leaving aside weird faces, people had their dogs, nails, rings and what not as their display pictures. Only about five people had their faces clearly visible in the pictures. Was I supposed to imagine their faces through the faces of their dogs?!

After another five minutes of 'where-am-I-stuck', I finally saw a recognizable face coming along with two unknown ones. They occupied an empty table near the window. I walked up to them.

"Are you guys from *DU Times*?" I asked.

"Yes," Recognizable Face replied.

"Hey. I am Avantika. I have been recruited recently," I said.

"Oh! Hi! Come, sit," the other person said.

I sat down. Random conversations continued till some more people arrived.

A dusky, slim and short girl arrived. On being seated, I was the first person she addressed.

She asked, "You must be Avantika?"

I replied, "Yes."

"I already met the other new recruits. We had an introductory meeting before you joined. I am the editor, Kashish."

I replied, "Oh, okay. Hello!"

I didn't know what to talk about, so I was quiet while the rest talked. Also, trust me, I had no idea what they were talking about most of the time. I hadn't even heard the names of the people they were talking about.

The editor said, "So, while we wait for the others, let us introduce ourselves."

She seemed nice, very down-to-earth and everybody kept teasing her for one reason or the other. In fact, everyone was friendly, trying to mix well with the group.

"Let's start with you." One of the guys pointed towards Kashish.

"Hello people. I am Kashish. Miranda House. Economics Hons. 3rd year."

"Hey I am Kamya. Venky. English Hons. 2nd year."

And the introductions went on, while the late comers occupied their places.

At 12.30 p.m., work began on a serious note. Kashish took out a diary and started writing headings like Page 1, Page 2 till Page 10, leaving gaps in between. Distribution work concerning event coverage was assigned to the people and those who were left were asked about the topics they were going to write on. Page 1 and page 2 were dedicated to news and events. Page 3 and 4 to interviews and advertisements. Page 5 had opinions. Page 6 was dedicated to pictures capturing the essence of life in the university. Page 7 and 8 contained reviews of books, shows, movies, food and games. Page 9 had fun activities like puzzles, horoscopes, etc. Page 10 was for sports lovers.

In addition to this, articles were required for the website too.

Those who were asked about the topics they would write on chose things from Page 3 to 10. They gave the names of the books, shows, movies, food places and games they were interested in reviewing. If something was not good enough to be reviewed, it was rejected. If there was a conflict between people regarding a topic, the majority votes decided the outcome. The content for the first two pages was decided on the basis of the events that people reported. Since almost everyone who was a part of the DUT Team came from major colleges, the events around the campus were easily put on the table. If someone was unable to cover an event for some reason, the responsibility was given to some other individual. Our articles were edited by copy editors before getting printed.

As a new recruit, having nothing major to contribute and still understanding the process of work, when I was asked about what I was going to write, I went for an opinion. I had not thought about the topic for the opinion till then and was not expecting to be asked, but then I was.

"E-books vs Paper Books" I said. Nothing else came into my mind at that point of time.

"Okay."

It was approved. A nice start!

As I put forward my topic, I saw a really handsome boy coming towards our table.

"Heya..." he greeted everyone.

Someone shouted, "Anuraaaag!"

So his name was Anurag.

He pulled a chair and sat by the editor's side. We were facing each other, so when he smiled at me, I smiled back. He asked the boy sitting next to him if he was an old member of the team. The boy replied in the negative. That meant that Anurag was new too. He was a lively person, talking to everybody around, cracking jokes and he landed with an article on sports. We were given deadlines for our work, taking into account the time that was required for designing and printing the paper. After the allotments were made, which took about 45 minutes, the meeting ended with an announcement that the next meeting would be held on 3 January, which was a Tuesday. The subsequent meetings would follow every Tuesday.

My driver was accompanying me that day, though I had learnt to drive, the reason being the unavailability of the driving license and lack of sufficient practice on my part.

I was waiting for my driver who had parked the car a little away from the venue. I was looking towards my right, anticipating the car's arrival on the one way road. I saw a car stopping about a metre away from me. Suddenly, Anurag emerged. He was moving towards that car. He got into the back seat and saw me standing.

"Should I drop you somewhere?" he asked.

He had also come with a driver. Such a handsome guy was asking me for a ride. How could I say no? But of course, I had to.

"No, thanks. I am waiting for my driver," I said.

"Oh, okay! Cool. See you," he said and left.

The rest of my days were spent writing articles, reading, driving and exercising. Initially, it took me about an hour to write an article. I wanted each line to smell like a fresh rose. I was sent various links of events for web reports. Such reports consumed about two hours since they required research, editing and contacting the people involved in the event. Converting the data into the required word limit demanded an extensive study. But looking at the bright side, I was now much more aware about the happenings in Delhi University.

The last twelve days were also marked by an embarrassing event. Anamika had sent me a link, asking me to take a look at a profile picture. It was Keith sir's profile, again. But this time, the focus was on Raghav sir. Raghav sir was the cute professor of our department, Keith sir being the handsome one. Keith sir had uploaded a picture with Raghav sir, in which, for a change, Raghav sir was looking better. As I was checking his profile on my phone, suddenly my phone slipped from my hands. Thanks to my reflexes, I was able to grab hold of it before it hit the floor but in this desperate attempt, I touched the 'Add friend' link on my phone. Touch screen phones, I tell you! I felt embarrassed. I was thinking about whether to cancel the request or not, while I continued checking his profile further. He would get a notification saying that Avantika Sareen had sent him a friend request and would later learn that I had cancelled it. Wouldn't that be more embarrassing than sending the request? And even if I had sent it, even though by mistake, what was the big deal? He had many students in his friends' list. I was debating the pros and cons in my head when I saw 'Keith Joseph has accepted your request' in the new notifications tab. That was quick.

If I would have cancelled the request in those few minutes, it would have been more embarrassing. Thinking about what just happened, I closed the app in a hurry.

Did you see? Anamika pinged.

Yes, I replied.

Do you keep checking Keith sir's profile every day? Do you have a crush on him? I added.

Lol. No, no. I was going to Raghav sir's profile through his and then I saw the picture. Raghav sir was looking so cute.

Yes, I replied.

I didn't tell her about this 'accident'. I was worried about facing Mr Joseph in college now. What impression did he form about me after visiting my profile, if he did so, was the thought that troubled me along with the thought about the impression I made by sending him a friend request.

•

New Year was here. I had a party on New Year's eve. Two of my school friends had come to my house for a night stay and we had a great time with lots of dancing, eating and drinking cold drinks. I was burning calories by dancing and gaining them simultaneously by drinking and eating. Every friend with whom I had lost contact sent me New Year wishes. But the one whom I was closest to at some point of time, Aarav, did not. I was reminded of the days which were gone.

My thoughts went back to the first day of the year which had ended a few hours back. Nobody was at home then. My mother had gone out for some work and so had my father. I was alone and really wanted to meet Aarav on the first day of the New Year. I had called him to come over and he had agreed. I wanted to look my best. I rushed towards the door after cleaning my room, as I heard the doorbell ringing. I hugged him before he could enter.

He laughed.

"What?" I asked.

"Allow me to come in at least," he replied.

I laughed, pulled him in and bolted the door. He pulled me towards him and lifted me.

"Shall we proceed?" he asked.

"No. Put me down first," I asked

"Nope," he said.

"I am heavy!" I said.

"No, you are not," he replied.

I loved it when he lifted me unexpectedly. I did not want to get down. I could spend a lifetime staying like that.

"I want to make coffee for you. You have never had anything made by me. Please put me down," I said. "Please…"

"Okay. Let me take you to the kitchen then," he said.

He took me to the kitchen and put me down.

I took a glass, poured some water into it and handed it over to him.

"Thought I would get coffee," he said in a musical tone.

"Yes, you will," I replied in the same tone.

I started making coffee for him. As I finished making a cup of coffee, he hugged me from behind. I could not move. He rotated me towards his side, my face in his hands and cuddled my nose with his. He kissed me on the forehead. My eyes were closed the entire time. I hid my face in his chest and he covered me with his jacket. He played with my hair and pulled my cheeks while my head rested on his chest.

I felt as if no evil power could come close to me, no negativity could look me in the face as he was there to protect me. He was my saviour. His warmth, his scent, his arms and his love were the only treasure that mattered to me. The sense of security I felt in his arms was unparalleled. I could experience eternity in just a second. My whole world, the reason for my existence, my guardian angel, it was all him. Only him. He could turn my demons into angels.

He kissed my head after we had remained in that position for about two minutes. He touched my chin and took my name. I looked up. He looked into my eyes and said,

"Avni, I love you."

I replied, "I love you too."

He kept staring at me. I blushed and looked down. He smiled and reached for the cup of coffee. After having a sip, he exclaimed,

"Not that bad!"

I smiled.

"Didn't you make a cup for yourself?" he asked.

I shook my head.

He laughed and asked me to share from his cup.

He took me to my room, placed the coffee cup on the side table and we sat on the bed.

"Is the coffee not good?" I asked.

"It is neither good nor bad," he answered.

"Okay," I said in a low voice.

He could make out that I was sad. He came near to me, brought his mouth next to my ears and whispered,

"It is the best coffee that I've ever tasted, Avni."

I blushed.

I said, "You are saying this to make me feel good, aren't you?"

He said, "No, Avni. I know whatever you do for me, you do it with all your heart. I know you want to give me the best of everything and I could clearly see that while I watched you make this coffee for me. This coffee has the best aroma and the best taste I've ever come across. Trust me."

"I love you, Aarav."

He drank the coffee and we lay down on the bed. I rested my head on his right arm.

"Have you made any New Year resolution?" I asked, twisting towards his side.

"No. Have you?"

"Yes," I said, putting my chin on his chest.

"What?" he asked.

"I won't tell you until you make a resolution of my choice," I said.

"And what is that?"

"That you will always be there by my side and will never leave me," I said.

He said, fiddling with my fingers, "Okay, ma'am."

"I want you to say that," I said, playing with his hair.

"I'll always be there by your side and will never leave you," he said, with love and affection in his eyes and voice. He pulled me towards him and kissed me.

We stayed there for an hour, next to each other, talking about our future, teasing each other until his phone rang and he was called home.

Who would've thought then, that a day would arrive when we would not even talk to each other? That all the words he spoke meant nothing to him while they meant the world to me. That everything was a lie.

In compensation, this 1 January brought with it a different kind of freedom. I received my driving licence and was all set to start the new session in college.

Genesis

I drove to college alone for the first time. I had gone there at least three times while practising but I was extra cautious that day since I didn't have dad by my side. I made it safely to college and didn't encounter much traffic as it was fairly early. I loved the experience and felt independent as never before.

I went to the room which was allotted to our class. I found many of my classmates already there. So I guess I wasn't the first one to arrive this time. Chit chats, hugs and taking pictures were the highlights of the day. I had received a message from the DUT Team asking me to collect the newspapers from the college gate at 10.00 a.m. I was so excited. An article in the newspaper under my name. It felt like a victory of some sort. I giggled about the fact that Tuesday could well be my new favourite day. I had told all my friends about my selection in the editorial team of DUT.

With immense excitement, I picked up the newspapers and the first thing I did after picking them up was to check page 5. Anamika and Ritvik read the entire article while walking and complimented me. I was giggling at the thought of showing the newspaper to my parents. I had shown them my articles online but getting something published in a newspaper was something entirely different. Seeing my name printed under the heading 'DUT Team' in the newspaper made me ecstatic. When my classmates got to know about it, some were not so happy, or jealous I think, and the others, genuinely happy. Unlike pity, jealousy has to be earned and I had earned it.

Keith sir and Raghav sir were teaching us this semester as well. My favourite teacher had recovered from the accident and was ready to join us. After giving a treat to my friends for my selection and a ride in my new car, I rushed to my second meeting. With the commencement of classes, meetings were to be a part of my weekly schedule and fortunately, I did not encounter Keith sir in college.

I did not know the route to Connaught Place from my college. My dad had advised me to take the route to CP after coming back to our locality since he feared that I would get lost even when he had explained the route from my college. I followed his advice. Finding a parking space is always a pain in the ass and this time was no different. It took me about ten minutes to find a decent parking space. I found one, nevertheless. The meeting went off well. I got a food review this time. So, I could try a new eating place without feeling guilty about the calories I was going to intake. It was my duty. Anurag had conveniently abstained himself from the meeting under some pretext which I couldn't hear properly when the seniors were talking about him.

The first thing I did after reaching home was to text Dad that I had reached safely and the second was to show the newspaper to my mother. She rarely praised me for my capabilities, but this wasn't one such time. In return, I asked her to make me a grilled sandwich and she readily obliged.

My dad said that he was proud of me when I showed him the article at night. He asked about my driving experience and we talked for half an hour about this and that. Our driver had not lost his job. He was put on dad's duty until the next month, in case I found driving inconvenient.

The next day I reached college earlier than I had expected. I had left home pretty late and was the first one to enter the class. I thought I had developed a new skill, 'panic driving', which actually made me drive faster than expected. I stayed inside the classroom as it was cold outside. I was checking my Facebook account when Mr Joseph entered the classroom. Maybe he had used his 'panic driving' skills as well!

"Good morning ," he greeted me.

"Good morning, sir."

"So, am I five minutes early again?" he asked, while adjusting his watch.

"No, I'm on time. Where are the others?" he asked.

"Must be on their way," I said.

"Where do you come from?" he asked.

"Defence Colony," I answered.

"Oh! That is far off. It must be arduous for you to come for early morning classes. I come from Civil Lines and find early morning classes extremely strenuous," he said, making a tired face.

I laughed.

"How do you come? The metro?" he asked.

"In my car," I answered.

"You drive?" he asked.

"Yes, sir."

I wanted to add that I had started driving to college only from the day before, but I did not.

"Oh! Great. I don't drive to college but don't use the metro either. It's laborious to first go to the metro station from home and then come to college from the station," he said.

I smiled. I wanted to ask him the reason for not driving to college but didn't have the courage. I kept thinking if it was due to his legs. My thoughts were dismissed soon when he asked, "So, do you actually like the course you've enrolled into, after a semester of experience?" he asked.

I explained, "I'm split into two, sir. I am from a Science background and scored really well in the board exams. But people close to me think that I've not made the right decision. They were not happy about my decision and the many arguments which I hear against my choice make me doubt it. Sometimes, I regret it too. But as far as I am concerned, I took Literature because I wanted to study just that. I feel lucky because I got the chance to study a subject of my choice and that too, in a prestigious college. I got what I desired in one sense, even if that desire was wrong according to people. I will have the chance to cover the three spheres of education: Science, Literature and Philosophy. I've studied Science, I'm pursuing Literature and Phi losophy will be one of the disciplines in the upcoming semesters. Most people don't get a chance to do so or pursue what they desire. My parents have always supported my decision. They wanted me to act as per my desire, not interfering in my studies. But yes, I miss Science too, even though I like Literature."

He said, "I get it."

He was going to say something and I wanted to listen to his thoughts about my choice, when we were interrupted by other students, asking for permission to get in. Those who commuted via the metro usually came in a bunch. Many students had entered in this round and the topic of our discussion lay dormant after that moment. The lecture began shortly after. Nothing much took place in college except that I bought my second semester books and tried a new food joint for the food review, before heading home.

The week was about to come to an end. Two days had passed since I had had the early morning chat with Mr Joseph. I wanted to go somewhere that day especially since the weather was rather pleasant. But all the nearby areas had already been trodden upon. My friends weren't ready to travel far as it had started raining, so I had to head back home. While I was going towards the parking area, it began pouring heavily. As I was about to sit inside my car, I saw Keith sir coming. He was about to fall down. He had slipped but regained his balance. I knew that he could take care of himself. As I was watching him, he noticed me.

He waved, "Hi."

Coming towards me, he stood by my side and said, "I was looking for public transport but couldn't find any due to the rain. So I decided to wait under a tree."

I had not noticed that I was standing under a tree until then. I smiled.

He asked, "Going home?"

"Yes."

He asked, "Remember the conversation that we were having that day?"

"Yes, sir," I replied, smiling. "I have something to add."

"Yes sure," he said, laughing.

"Literature students are always short of marks. Seeing my first semester results makes me long for Science," I said, laughing.

He asked, "How much did you score?"

"I scored a 69 percent. I've never scored less than 90 percent my entire student life. This was disheartening."

"Sixty-nine percent in first semester in Literature is good. See, you don't get full marks in literature, so the percentage is always on the lower side. Anybody who has knowledge of the subject knows that. So you need not worry," he said.

I said, "Yes, that's true."

"And I'm guessing you would be the topper of your class," he added.

"Yes."

I had topped in the first semester. To my parents, it was nothing new. They were not excited to a great extent after hearing this news. It didn't affect me either.

"See. Told you. Listen to me, Avantika. Whatever you do, be the best in that field. Nothing else matters. When you look up at the blue sky and see white dots flying around, you actually see your own white blood cells. That is a reflection of your own being. It is only your opinion which should matter, not others'. It is your own self which should be looked upon for inspiration, strength and judgment. Take your own decisions, irrespective of others' beliefs."

I nodded.

He said, "You must be getting late. You can go. I'll leave as soon as I find some conveyance."

"Do you want me to drop you? Civil Lines is on my way."

I lied. It wasn't. I didn't know how I gathered the courage to ask my professor if I could drop him to his house. Maybe the source of this courage was his inspiring words.

He asked, "Is it?"

"Yes," I lied again. It was a noble lie.

"Don't worry. I'll go on my own," he said.

"I don't drive that badly, sir," I said, smiling.

He laughed and agreed to come with me.

I didn't want to leave him alone, struggling to find transport in the heavy downpour. This wish gave a convincing strength to my voice, which couldn't have been possible under any normal circumstances.

"So how big is your family?" he asked while we were on our way.

"Only my parents. No siblings," I answered.

"So, you've been in Delhi since your childhood?" he asked.

"Yes sir."

He told me that he was from Bangalore.

I asked, "Do you miss Bangalore?"

"Umm... not really. I graduated from Hans Raj. When I was studying, I used to live as a paying guest. Now, I live in a flat. During my graduation, my sister wasn't married so I missed Bangalore but she's married now, and has shifted to Nainital. I have nobody there. My parents had died in an accident. Moreover, I am used to Delhi now," he said.

I said, "Oh, okay!"

He asked, "What do you do apart from studying? Any specific interests?"

I answered, "I read, write and do random things."

"You write? What do you write about?" he asked.

"Poems. At the professional level, articles for *DU Times*. I've been recruited recently. Have you seen that newspaper in college?" I said.

"Yes, I have. Good. I like that you're doing something meaningful."

"Thank you, sir," I said.

"And what do you read?" he asked.

We were about to reach our destination when he asked this.

"I like Gabriel Garcia Marquez. Have you read anything written by him?" he added.

"Yes, I have. I've read *Love in the Time of Cholera*. I am looking forward to read *One Hundred Years of Solitude*," I said.

He replied, "Oh! That is an amazing book."

I said, "Amitav Ghosh is my favourite, in general. But I like Gabriel's work too."

"Amitav Ghosh is good too. I like that guy. Do you know that he's coming to Stephen's tomorrow?" he asked.

"I heard that he was coming but didn't know that it was tomorrow," I said.

There was a discussion in the last meeting of the *DU Times* about Amitav Ghosh coming to talk to the students as he was an alumnus of St. Stephen's College. The exact date had not been decided till then and a guy from Stephen's had volunteered to cover it. He had been invited by the literary society of the college.

"It is tomorrow. You should go. I am thinking of attending it too. Anyway, you can drop me here," Mr Joseph said.

I said, "It's okay. I can drop you somewhere close to your house. It is still raining."

We were at a red light at that time.

"No, I don't want you to get lost in the lanes. Take a left turn from here and you'll reach the main road. See you," he said getting out of the car.

He did the right thing. I would have definitely lost my way. I was glad he told me about the left turn!

●

I asked my friends if they would like to attend Amitav Ghosh's talk. Anamika agreed. Ritvik was busy as he was a part of a college society and fests were round the corner. Manvika was out of town.

I woke up in the morning, only to read a text message. Anamika had suddenly fallen sick. She would not be able to attend the talk or come to college, she had texted. And she was feeling really bad about it but couldn't convince her mother to let her attend the talk. I thought that I'd not go to college either after reading the message as it was extremely disheartening. But, the hope of finding someone in college who would accompany me, made me change my mind.

Unfortunately, those who were there in class weren't interested or were busy or didn't want to miss classes. Half of the class was out of town and was to return in the following week, so there weren't many students present in the class. According to a message in the DUT group, the talk was to start at 1.00 p.m., which meant being inside the hall at 12.30 p.m. I was expecting a few people to be interested, but they were absent. Maybe they would go to the talk directly and not come to college, I thought. Whatever the case, I had company until morning, but not anymore.

I was passing the staff room to go to the room where the next class was scheduled when I ran into Keith sir.

"Are you going for the talk?" he asked.

"I want to, but I don't have company," I said.

"Same here. Since it's a Saturday, many teachers of our department are absent. They have an off day. The present ones are busy, in classes and otherwise. I'm the only one who'll be free before twelve," he said.

"Aren't the students interested? I thought they would be enthusiastic."

I said, "All of them have their reasons for not going. I was really enthusiastic. I have even got a book written by him to get it signed."

"That's great. When do your classes get over?" he asked.

"Late afternoon. At 2.30 p.m. If I decide to attend the talk, I'll miss them," I said.

"You should attend it, without second thoughts. If you need company, I can accompany you. I'll go alone too, so we can go with each other and let Mr Ghosh know how his books have inspired the students and teachers alike," he said.

Wow! A date? No, not really!

"Okay, sir. I'll meet you at the college gate at 12.20 p.m. It's just across the street so we can leave that late."

"Yes, yes. Perfectly fine. See you then. And if more people are interested, bring them with you. We can all go together," he said.

"Okay, sir. See you."

This was going to be a first. Hanging out with a professor! Life was really changing.

I met Keith sir at the decided time.

"Nobody came along?" he asked.

I shook my head.

"Nevermind. Let's go," he said. I followed him.

We were seated by 12.30 p.m. We talked about books and movies which were based on novels till Mr Ghosh arrived. He was a little late but it was okay. Mr Joseph and I got some time to catch up. I had never thought that I could be so friendly with a professor. I shared my future plans and discussed issues with teachers in school and there were some of them whom I really liked, but hadn't thought that I could share a higher level of comfort with a college professor. Life is full of surprises!

We stopped chatting when Mr Ghosh arrived. The silence between us didn't break till he left. It was an hour-long talk. Mr Ghosh talked about his life and his book *The Shadow Lines* which was a prescribed text in the second semester, which meant that I was going to have to read it too. I had not read the text till then, so I had no clue about the questions the students were asking him, regarding the book. From what I could gather, I could make out that the students were really disheartened about the death of a character named Tridib. A person even went on to suggest that the book should be re-printed with an alternate ending, the one in which Tridib lives. Such was the level of attachment book lovers develop with the characters! Mr Joseph and Mr Ghosh both laughed at the suggestion. I laughed too, even though I hadn't read the book. He answered everyone's questions and seemed a really nice person.

After the talk was over, many wanted to get the books signed by Mr Ghosh.

"Go, join the line. Get your book signed. I am waiting for you here," Mr Joseph urged me to go.

I did as instructed.

It was a long queue so it took about fifteen minutes to get the book signed. When I was standing in the queue, it suddenly struck me that Keith sir was the one who would teach us this book. He was talking about it in his last class. I had completely forgotten about that. My favourite male professor was going to teach the book written by my favourite author! Time to start concentrating in his classes more and probably start sitting in the first row, were my thoughts.

I got my book signed and returned to Mr Joseph. He was standing with Raghav sir. Wait! What?

"Good afternoon, sir," I greeted him.

He greeted me back.

More teachers of our department joined us. But that wasn't the end of it. I saw some of my classmates too. They were standing opposite us. I didn't want them to see me lest I might be asked questions regarding who I was with.

"Sir, I've to go. Can I leave?" I said, looking at Mr Joseph.

"Yes, of course. Did you like the talk?" he asked.

I said, "Yes, I did. I will start reading this text as soon as I get home."

He said, "You better do that. I am teaching this book. Remember?"

To this, Raghav sir laughed. I took leave and left, without being seen by my classmates.

Book hangovers were common. 'Meeting hangovers' only happened in Aarav's case. That day saw a new addition in the latter list. I kept thinking about each word that Keith sir and I had exchanged. He was an interesting individual, had wide-ranging interests, was good at heart and was supportive. He was a person whom I could bond with and talk endlessly about various things. I was beginning to think that we were first friends, student and professor later. Irritated by my thoughts, I decided to finish reading *The Shadow Lines* in one go. If I made up my mind to do something, I would usually complete it in one go. Nothing could distract me then.

Book hangovers are more fun than the alcohol ones. They take you into a completely different world. You don't call your ex-es, you just forget them. You even forget your world, regret something that has happened in a different world, praise a character that you may never find in the real world, fall in love with a character outside the realm of ordinary existence, experience pain for someone else. This pain is what makes you stick to your humanity, away from the inhumane world. These hangovers don't numb the mind. They open it to imagination and to reality. I knew many worlds better than reality and that they existed in books.

Declaration of Love

It was a Sunday afternoon. I had finished reading the book by the morning. I loved it. I was feeling feverish though. I checked my temperature with a thermometer only to find the mercury touching the 102 degree mark. Even though I had taken some medicines, the fever had not subsided by the day after, so I didn't go to college.

Having nothing better to do at home, I spent my time gossiping with mom. It wasn't easy to make us stop once we started. There wasn't any need to stop that day, either.

"Mom, do you remember that dream which I used to have?" I asked my mom.

She asked, "Which one?"

"The one in which there was a red and white building? Or a fort? Or whatever?" I replied.

"Yes, I remember. Why?"

"I've been having that dream again, lately. I had it about two or three times in the last month and one yesterday. Exactly the same dream with the same place, same act, same time frame, same colours, same everything!"

"People who play video games frequently, are more likely to have the ability to control their dreams. Maybe I should start playing video games now!" I joked.

"This is weird. Do you think a lot about that dream?" she asked.

"Nope," I replied.

"Are you stressed about something? Do you want to share anything with me?" she went on asking.

"No, Mom. I share everything with you. I have nobody to share things with, except you. You know everything. But I am annoyed at having the same dream again and again. This happens only in movies, you know. It is strange."

"Yes, it is. I will talk to your dad about this. We will consult somebody."

"No. Don't tell dad about this. It's just a stupid dream," I said.

"But it is getting me worried," she said.

"Don't get worried. It's just a dream. It cannot possibly kill me," I said. "You know what! I am happy that I have fever. At least, I didn't have to wake up early and go to college."

"Why can't you say something good?" she asked, being irritated.

"Come on, Mom! You know how lazy I am and waking up early during the winters when it is dark, when even the sun hasn't risen completely, is torturous!"

"You can never change. Do you want anything to drink, tea or coffee?" she asked.

"Coffee."

•

It was Wednesday evening. I had been skilfully avoiding visiting the doctor but my dad would hear none of it now. My health wasn't improving. I had to go see the doctor.

The doctor recommended some blood tests. He gave me some medicines as well. The next day my parents took me for the tests.

I wasn't looking at the syringe, but I could feel my energy withering away. Each drop of blood which was transferred from my veins to the syringe left me with a sense of something leaving my body. My energy level deteriorated with every drop. It was as if someone was taking my soul away from my body. It was scary.

After the required amount of blood was taken, I started feeling dizzy. My mom noticed it and asked me to sit down on one of the benches in the room. My mother always carried a packet of biscuits and water with glucose mixed in it, whenever anyone from our family went for a blood test. She asked me to have a sip of that water. I did as she said, but it didn't help. My vision started getting blurred, the noise around me was slowly fading and I was losing consciousness. Since it was a small closed room, my father asked my mother to take me to the outer lobby for fresh air so that I didn't feel suffocated. They took me outside. I was seated on a chair which was placed in the outer lobby. I saw my dad saying something to my mom. He went out after that. I could hear no more. I couldn't hear what he had just said. My mother pointed towards the fan and said something. I didn't respond. She wiped my face with a cloth. She kept fanning my face and in a few minutes, I regained consciousness. My vision cleared and I could hear the noise around. My dad had brought the car at the gate. As soon as I sat inside the car, I felt okay. We reached home quickly. Mom asked me to lie down and rest. Dad came inside my room and asked us not to worry.

"Don't worry. Everything will be clear once the reports come out. They will be handed over to us by the evening. All the tests will be covered. You'll be fine. Eat well and rest."

I nodded.

The reports came out in the evening. Nothing that the doctor had feared was detected but my haemoglobin count was really low. It was just 9.8 or something. Everything else was fine. The doctor asked us to continue the medicines he had given the last time. When my dad questioned him about my condition after giving blood, he said it was not something to be worried about, as some people feel anxiety under such circumstances. He had, of course, commented upon my HB count, but assured us that nothing major had happened to me. After we reached home, my dad handed over a diet chart for me to follow to raise my HB count. I was given several instructions. My mom's face conveyed everything. She didn't say anything but I could tell that she was worried, extremely worried.

At around 9.00 p.m. I received a message from Keith sir.

Avantika, tell your classmates that I won't take the class tomorrow.

Okay, sir. I replied.

Oh by the way, I hope you did not take my words seriously. I didn't mean that you shouldn't attend classes till you've read the book completely. LOL

I've read the book, sir. Was not well so couldn't come for classes, I wrote.

He asked, *What happened?*

Fever.

Oh okay. Take care.

I replied with a smiley.

It is said that a crush lasts only four months. If it exceeds that time, then you're in love. By that reckoning, I was already in love with Mr Joseph!

After the exchange of messages, I was about to tell other students about Keith sir's class, when I received a message from him.

I've told the other CR of your class to convey the message. You take rest. Get well soon.

I replied, *Okay. Thanks sir.*

I hoped he doesn't relieve me of my CR duties permanently!

Seven days passed and I was well enough to step out of my home and go to college. I was forbidden to drive. Not letting go of the driver turned out to be a wise idea. I had missed out on the Tuesday meetings during the course of my sickness, but the editor was aware of my poor health. She had asked me to take care of myself. I took with myself lots of fruits in my bag. I had trouble understanding what was being taught in classes, but hadn't missed too much. Keith sir seemed happy to see me in his class. He had classes four days a week, so I hoped he might have missed seeing my face.

It had rained that day. After the classes got over, I headed straight towards my car. Climbing down the stairs, which were slippery, I lost my balance and slipped. I was talking to Manvika who was behind me. I had hurt myself a little as I fell down. Anamika and Manvika helped me out.

"Avantika, you're hurt!" Anamika said.

"Do you have a handkerchief?" she asked Manvika.

I was bleeding.

"I have it," I handed over the handkerchief to her. She wiped away my blood but it kept flowing.

"Manvika, take out the water bottle from Avantika's bag," Anamika instructed.

Manvika handed over the bottle to her. She poured a little water on the handkerchief which was stained with blood – the sight of which was making me feel uncomfortable – and applied it on the bruised area.

"Come, Avantika. Your wound needs to be dressed. We'll take you to the medical room," Anamika said.

We went to the medical room. It was closed.

"I can't wait, Anamika. I can't stand. I need to get back home. My driver is accompanying me. By the time this room gets opened, I'll be home," I said.

"Okay. We'll drop you to the gate," she replied.

I called my driver when we were on our way to the college gate. He had gone somewhere else to eat. He said that it would take a little time for him to come to the gate.

"Is your driver coming?" Manvika asked.

"Yes. He's on his way." As I said this, I heard the rumbling of thunder in the sky.

"You two can leave. It's going to rain again. You guys go now or else you'll get drenched," I said.

"No, we can wait."

"My driver is on his way. You don't need to worry. You should leave, guys," I said.

"Are you sure?" Anamika asked.

"Yes."

Manvika handed over my bag to me and they left. I removed my handkerchief from the wound to see if it was still bleeding. It was. The sight of blood caused a strange feeling in me. I started feeling anxious. I couldn't bear to stand. My legs refused to support my body. I consoled myself that it was just a matter of a few minutes, but my body gave up. My vision started blurring and I collapsed.

When I opened my eyes, I was lying on a bench. I looked around. I was in a classroom. Keith sir was sitting by my side.

"Avantika, are you okay? What happened to you? Why were you bleeding?" he hurled down the questions upon me as he saw my eyes opening slowly.

"I am fine, sir," I said.

"Who told you to stand there while you were bleeding? What were you doing? You should have told someone who could have helped you. You should have told me. Why didn't you let me know?"

The concern was noticeable in his voice. The terror that is born out of the fear of losing someone close to you, someone you value – a feeling of genuine concern.

"Do you realize how much blood you've lost?" he continued.

"It's just a small wound, sir. It doesn't matter. I am alive," I said, getting up.

"Sit, Avantika. How could you say that? Do you even know how seeing you in this condition makes me feel? What matters is that I was worried about you when you stopped coming to college, what matters is that you haven't even recovered completely and you have been bleeding badly. What matters is that today was the first day of college after a whole week and you've hurt yourself already! Seeing you suffer makes me suffer. Why don't you get it, Avantika? I can't bear to see you like this. I want to see you happy, smiling, chirping, playing! I love you, damn it!"

He spoke everything in just a single breath. Every word that he said highlighted the struggle he was having within himself. He spoke as a dying man would, when a knife has been thrust upon his heart. The sense of urgency was clear in his speech. His emotions were true. They conveyed the truth that lay hidden in his soul. I could feel the pain in his voice. I felt that pain with him.

"What did you say, sir?" I wanted to make sure that what I heard was true – that he loved me.

"Nothing. I said nothing," he said these words as if he had just woken up from a dream.

"Sir…" I was going to say something when he cut me short.

"Avantika, I think you should go back home now. It is pretty late. The medical room is closed so I can't take you there."

As he said this, he moved as if to leave.

As he spoke, I got up.

"I won't leave until you repeat what you had said," I said, firmly.

"Leave Avantika!" he shouted.

I didn't budge an inch. He started walking. He had taken a few steps when he looked back at me. I hadn't moved.

"We will talk about that later. You are not well. You are not in the condition to talk. Please go home," he said.

"I am in the condition to talk about it, sir." I asserted.

"Please, Avantika. Try to understand. You need to go home. I promise you, we will talk about it. Trust me," he pleaded.

I nodded.

I took out my phone to call my driver. There were sixteen missed calls and three messages. My driver and my parents had called and left messages. My phone was on vibration mode which was why I had not heard it. I called my driver and asked him to come to the gate. I called my dad as I was leaving the room. Keith sir followed me to the gate.

"Where are you? Are you okay? Where was your phone?" my dad questioned me.

"Sorry Dad. I was in a class. My phone was on silent. I saw your message and missed calls just now."

I lied.

"Oh, thank god! I was so worried. I'll tell your mom. She had been trying your phone too. Go home now," he said.

"Yes, I'm going," I said and hung up.

"Why did you lie to your dad?" Mr Joseph asked.

"I'll tell my parents after I reach home. I didn't want them to worry about me."

We reached the gate. My driver was waiting for me. I went my way and he went his.

"You had asked me to come to the gate earlier. Where were you?" my driver asked as I stepped inside the car.

"I had some work," I said.

I was glad he hadn't noticed my wound. I didn't want to answer anyone's questions. I wanted some peace and to remain quiet.

I was asked a dozen questions about my wound once I got home. I had lost a significant amount of blood. All the more reason to allow the stress to creep in as my HB count was already low. I was feeling weak, sick and lethargic. The doctor advised bed rest for the next three to four days. I took a lot of heat from my parents because they thought that I had been careless while climbing down the stairs. I would have to be in bed for more days. I regretted saying that I liked to be sick. I was worried about my new job as I was going to miss the next meeting too. I expressed my gratefulness to god that they tested the new recruits on the basis of the first three months so I had a lot of time to cover up and do well. My low HB count made me think that if a vampire was to suck my blood, he would rather collapse due to osmosis, caused by huge differences in our blood concentration levels!

Almost half of the month was spent in bed. On Monday evening, I received a message from Keith sir,

Hey! Are you okay? I blushed as I read the message.

Doctor has advised me bed rest.

Oh. Till when?

I will be back in college on Wednesday. This has been decided as of now.

Okay, take care.

We were supposed to talk about something.

Forget everything that happened that day. I didn't mean what I had said. I was too overwhelmed by emotions. There is nothing to talk about.

You had promised me. I trusted you, I replied.

We don't need to talk about it as I didn't mean what I said, he replied.

Don't lie.

Okay. If you don't want to tell the truth, which resonated so clearly in your voice, and don't want to talk about it, then don't. But I will not attend any of your classes until you fulfil your promise. I will come to college, attend all classes except yours. This is a promise. And unlike you, I don't break promises. I declared.

He did not reply to my message, but he had seen it.

I was attracted to him – the kind of attraction which you experience for a person because of the way he is. Neither did

I think about marrying him, nor about our future. I didn't want any physical intimacy with him. I just wanted to be with him. I liked spending time with him. I didn't know whether to call it love or not. What I knew was that this feeling was rare. I couldn't afford to lose him. Initially, I had liked him for his politeness but now, I liked him for his interests, thoughts, behaviour, opinions – for what he was, as a person.

I started going to college from Wednesday. My driver accompanied me. That week, I attended all classes except Keith sir's lectures. When he had an early morning class, I would go to college late. When he had a class during the day, I would miss it, making an excuse so that my friends didn't suspect that something was amiss. We would encounter each other in corridors, but I would look away. I would see him looking at me but I was stubborn and determined to stick to my word.

On Tuesday, when the classes got over and there was still time for the DUT meeting to start, I went to meet Keith sir in the staff room. He was doing some work and wasn't surrounded by teachers.

"Sir!" I said.

He looked at me.

"I wanted to tell you that I won't be able to carry out the duties of being the CR of your class from now on, since I would be unable to attend any future classes of yours due to personal reasons. Please appoint a new CR," I said.

"Wasn't Amitav Ghosh your favourite?" he asked. I was like, Seriously?!

"He still is," I answered and turned around to leave.

"Wait. I want to talk to you. Come with me."

He stood up. I followed him. He took me to a vacant classroom.

"Why are you doing this, Avantika? Think about your parents at least! You are missing out on your attendance. You won't get your admit card unless you have the required attendance. They won't let you appear for the exams." He was worried.

"I don't care, sir," I replied.

He sighed.

"What do you want to talk about?" he asked, frustratingly.

"I just want to tell you that I had heard what you had said that day and I feel the same for you," I replied.

"What? Do you understand the implication of your words, Miss Sareen?" he said.

"I do," I replied.

"No, you don't, because you wouldn't have said this if you really did," he said.

I didn't say anything, just stared at him.

"Avantika, whatever I said that day was a big mistake. I didn't want to say those things. I'm still angry at myself for what I said. I was just overwhelmed by emotions and didn't realise what I was saying."

I replied, "You don't need to be angry at yourself for what you had said that day. You need to blame yourself for what you're saying and doing now."

"Listen to me, Avantika. I am a professor and you are a student. This is the only relationship that is possible between us," he said.

"You are wrong, sir. This isn't the only kind of relationship we can have, between us. We are human beings first, and student and professor later," I replied.

"Do you even realise what you're saying? People will scorn at the idea of this kind of love," he said.

I said, "I don't care about what people think. I care about what I feel for you. I don't get into relationships because the public demands it; I get into a relationship when I want and need it."

I continued, "You and I weren't the ones who chose this path for ourselves. Destiny chose it for us. Destiny played its part when you couldn't find a mode of transport in the heavy rain, when we couldn't find anyone to accompany us for Amitav Ghosh's event, when I fainted and you were passing by. I wasn't the one who planned all this; nor did you. You can't decide the course of your actions on the basis of what people would like you to do. People are living their lives without keeping you in mind while making their choices. What do you think individuality is!"

He said, "And what about me being a man who limps while walking? I am twenty-nine. You are not even twenty. I am "disabled". You are perfect. You've a bright future in front of you. You are going to marry a worthy man and have a happy married life. I don't even know if I would ever marry someone!"

He had made very clear every reason due to which he thought we were incompatible in one go.

"It isn't about a man who limps while walking being in a relationship with a privileged girl. It isn't about an older man being in love with a younger girl. It isn't about a student having a relationship with a professor. It is about two individuals being in love with each other, two souls understanding each other, two humans admiring each other," I replied.

"Avantika, you will spoil your future," he protested.

"You are who you are. You are not old. You are just twenty-nine. Age difference doesn't matter when it comes to love. The society which you are talking about can offer ample examples of the same. We are two individuals trapped in social roles of a student and a professor. We can, of course, break away from these roles," I explained.

"Avantika, you don't understand…" as he was speaking, I cut him short.

"You are the one who needs to understand, not me. This kind of love and affection requires courage – courage to face the world, courage to fight the world for your love, courage to break free from the existing social norms, courage to show the society what love is, and courage to live for yourself. You know what your problem is? Your problem is not love; it is fear. You are scared. You are scared of going against the existing social conventions, of facing the world, of fighting for your rights. Many have done these things before you. They had the courage. They were not passive victims of the social code but active fighters asserting their individuality. You are a coward. I wouldn't like to be taught by a man who cannot face society and is spineless," I said.

As I said this, I began walking away from him.

"I am not scared for myself. I am scared for you. I am scared of the taunts you'll have to listen to, of the things you'll have to go through. Of your vivacity turning into silence," he spoke.

I stopped, turned around and walked towards him.

"Do you think I'll go around telling everyone about us? I am not stupid. I will not tell anyone anything. People will learn everything themselves," I said.

"And what after that? You'll complete your graduation and leave college. What future does our love promise?" he asked back.

"I am still in the first year. I don't know what's going to happen. You can't spoil your present worrying about the future. Maybe I'll be your M.A. student, who knows? Who says that we can't see each other when our student-teacher relationship ceases to exist?" I put forward my point.

He was silent. He said nothing in return.

"I don't want you to walk around the college campus holding my hand. I don't expect you to be all lovey-dovey like boyfriends are in general. I don't wish to receive flowers from you every day. I am not asking you to run around declaring that you're dating me! I just want you to not repress what you feel for me. I want you to tell me that you love me if you do, without giving a damn about what people would think. If you don't love me, say it. But, at least speak the truth. I want you to think of us as individuals. I want you to feel free, not bound by anything. If our love is coming in the way of your freedom, then tell me. I want you to be true to yourself and act as per your wishes. Of course, that doesn't apply to situations where mutual consent is required, but that mutual consent has to be between the people involved and not the whole world!"

I began moving towards the door. He was in a deep thought. He had nothing to say. As I was walking, I stopped. Without turning around, I said, "I'll be attending your classes from now onwards since you've fulfilled your promise of talking to me. Regarding your agreement on what I've just said, if it is a no, then you need to appoint some other CR in my place because I've been pretty irregular and wouldn't like to continue with the responsibility owing to my medical condition. If it's a yes, then you don't need to do that. Your next class will decide the outcome of our conversation. And I care about my parents. I wanted to see if you cared about me."

I left the room and went for the meeting.

The meeting went well. I was covering sports that week.

Union

"Good morning, everyone," Keith sir greeted the students as he entered the classroom for his next class.

All this while, every minute was spent in anticipation. I couldn't focus on anything. I waited impatiently for his next class but at the same time, I had my fears. What if everything was going to be over? What would happen to me if I was to love him forever? Would I be able to face him then? A million thoughts had passed through my mind.

"Good morning, sir," the students greeted him.

Everybody began to take out their books and started settling down. He was looking absolutely normal. He was behaving as though nothing had happened. I wondered if he remembered anything. He seemed to have forgotten everything. He didn't have a class the day before and so he had a day's time to think about us. My heart was thumping loudly as he entered the classroom. Somewhere deep inside, I knew that the decision could be laid bare before me anytime.

He began teaching. I couldn't concentrate. Was he going to say anything or not? Weird person!

I was struggling with my thoughts, thinking that confessing my love for him was the most foolish thing I could have done when like a bolt from the blue, he said, "Oh I forgot. I wanted to give you some handouts."

With this, he took out a thick bunch of papers.

"Avantika," he called out my name.

My heartbeat started beating faster.

"Since you are the CR of my class, please get these photocopied and circulate them in your class."

He declared that I was the CR. He had agreed. He wasn't going away from me.

He smiled at me as he looked towards me, handing over the handouts. I blushed and looked down. After a few seconds, I looked up. He was looking at me with a half-smile.

We exchanged glances throughout the rest of the class while he taught.

"Hello, Miss Sareen," Keith sir said as I stood behind him in the staff room.

There were teachers inside the room but none near him. He was occupied with work and was sitting alone.

"Hello, sir. How did you know it was me? I didn't even say a word."

"That is what love is, I guess," he said in a low voice so that people couldn't hear.

I handed over the handouts to him.

"Got them photocopied?" he asked.

"Yup," I answered.

"So fast. Why would someone want to change the CR when the present one is so efficient!" he smirked at me as he said this.

"Was that the only reason for not changing me, sir?" I asked.

"Not really. I had personal reasons which I wouldn't like to disclose in public," he said softly.

I smiled.

"Actually, it wasn't that fast. You gave them to me in the morning and it is afternoon now," I said.

He checked the time.

"Oh god! I have been so preoccupied with work, I lost track of time. I haven't even eaten anything since morning," he said.

"Oh! So are you done now? At what time do you get free?" I asked.

"Why? Do you want to talk about something, Miss Sareen?" he asked.

I loved the way he called me Miss Sareen. It was kind of seductive.

"No, my classes are over so I was thinking that I could drop you.. somewhere. It might rain, you know!" I said.

I grinned at him.

"I suppose your driver still accompanies you," he said, winking at me.

"Oh yes! I had completely forgotten about that! He accompanies me. How could I forget that!" I exclaimed.

He laughed. Getting up from his seat, he said, "I've one more class right now. I will see you later." I nodded and came out of the room with him. After that, I left for home after distributing the *DU Times*.

•

I wanted Mr Joseph to read my articles and comment on them. *DU Times* was distributed every Thursday. It was distributed on Monday only on the day when the new session began. In my absence, some other person was given the duty of distribution in our college. The article which I was given to write recently was to be published in the coming week's issue.

For the first time in my life after meeting Aarav, I was happy, glad, and ecstatic without him being the reason for it. I would smile and blush whenever I'd think of Mr Joseph. I wanted to talk to him 24x7, but didn't want to text him first. I didn't want to be annoying. I was full of energy, my face glowing, cheeks blossoming and suddenly the world had become a better place to live in. That is what love does to you. You become a happier person, the bitterness in your life starts diminishing and you let go of the grudges you had been holding for a long time. Everything seems renewed. You start imagining yourself with the person you love while listening to a romantic song. You laugh to get his or her attention. You draw silly hearts on sheets, joining his initials with yours. One person becomes the end of the world for you. And most importantly, you start living.

The exchange of glances, and sly smiles had become the order of the day since Thursday. I had attended all his classes but we had not talked for two days. On Saturday, all my friends were absent and I was rather bored. I suddenly remembered that Mr Joseph had told me that many teachers of our department had a day off on Saturday. Thinking that he might like my company, I went to the staff room when there was still time for the next class. He wasn't there. Dejected, I came out of the room. As I was trying to move out, a tall figure came in front of me, trying to get in. Without looking up, I moved towards the right, giving him space to get in. He too moved towards the right at the same time as I did. It happened once again, towards the left. Being rather annoyed, I looked up. It was him! He was smiling. My face lit up as soon as I saw that it was Mr Joseph.

"Umm... I just wanted to know if you have more handouts to give," I said, trying to conceal my joy.

"Umm...I guess not," he answered.

"Okay..." I said and kept standing there.

"Getting bored?" he asked, trying to look into my eyes.

"How do you know?" I asked.

"I can look at your face and know everything." He winked.

"Who are you? A face reader?" I asked.

"Umm... just yours," he answered.

I laughed.

"You want to talk, right?" he asked.

I nodded.

"Come. Let us go to some peaceful place," he said.

We went to the parking area and sat on one of the seating walls.

"So, tell me. How are you now?" he asked.

"I am good. Never felt better. You?" I replied.

"Same. Are your friends bunking college today?" he asked.

"They weren't in a mood to attend classes. I had to come because I've already missed a lot of classes this month," I answered.

"Hmm."

"So, do I get any advantage of being with my professor? Would you give me extra marks?" I joked, looking at his face for his reaction.

"Not at all, Miss Sareen. No advantages whatsoever," he replied.

"Okay, Mr Joseph. You live alone, right?" I asked.

"Yes."

"No pets?"

"No. Do you have any pets at home?" he asked back.

"No, but I do want a cat," I replied.

"Do you cook?" I asked.

"Yes. When I'm not well, I ask my maid, who does the other household work, to cook for me and I pay her extra for that," he replied.

"Oh great! You cook. What can you make?" I asked.

"Almost everything. I'll make something for you one day. You don't know how to cook, do you?" he asked.

"Nope," I answered.

As I said this, his phone rang. He had to leave for a meeting, so he apologised and turned away.

"Sir!" I called him from behind.

"Now you will not have to ask for help from your maid," I said.

He looked befuddled.

"Because now you can count on me. I will learn cooking... for you," I said.

He smiled and went away. Not much time was left for my next class, so I hurried towards the classroom.

On Thursday, I collected the newspapers, kept two for myself, and circulated the others. I went to the staff room. Unfortunately, there were other teachers around him. Not that they could stop me from meeting him.

"Sir, you had called me," I said.

"Me?" Keith sir asked.

He looked at me and I scrunched my eyes.

"Oh! Yes, yes! I did. Come outside," he said as he saw my expression.

"Clever trick, Miss Sareen," he complimented as we came outside the room.

"I wanted you to read something," I said.

"What?" he asked.

"Here," I said, handing over one of the newspapers to him.

"You can fold it and keep it in your pocket if you don't want your colleagues to notice. My articles have been published in it. Read them when you are free and tell me if you liked them, objectively," I said,

"Okay, ma'am," he replied.

"Good boy! I have to go now. Bye," I said.

Later in the day, I received a message from him.

I liked your articles. Nicely written. Well crafted. The points you put forth in the opinion section were well-researched. The review had all the important information that one would like to know. Good job. I like the way you write.

I thanked him. Unexpectedly, a chat followed after this which lasted for an hour. It was a happy end to a happy day.

Blossom

It was a cold Tuesday in February. My classes got over early so I decided to show my face at home before attending the DUT meeting. I had convinced dad to let me drive since it had been a month since I had fallen ill. He had agreed, though reluctantly. Also, this time, my driver wanted to leave for his village. I was about to sit inside the car when someone called my name. I recognized the voice. It was Mr Joseph.

"Going home?" he asked.

"Yes. No more classes. Had nothing to do so..." I answered.

"I was looking for you," he said.

"Why?" I asked.

"Wouldn't you ask me for a ride today? I cannot see your driver around," he replied.

"Yes, sure. Come in," I said, with a grin on my face.

Having said this, I began to turn around.

"Avantika!" he called me.

"Yes?" I asked.

"Actually, I wanted more than just a ride," he said.

I kept looking at him, impassively.

"I... I wanted to take you out for lunch... if you are fine with it," he said a little hesitatingly.

"No, Mr Joseph. I wanted to go home early."

I said and laughed on seeing his tensed face.

"I was kidding. Of course, I'm fine with it."

As I said this, a smile resurfaced on his face.

"Thank you, Miss Sareen," he said.

"Trust me, Mr Joseph, the pleasure is all mine. So where do you want to take me? Can we take the car?" I asked.

"Yes, I'll guide you," he said.

We sat inside the car and I drove as per his instructions.

"I had seen this place some days ago. I loved it so I wanted to show it to you," he said while we talked in the car.

"This was the reason why you were looking for me?" I asked.

"Yes."

"You could have just called or messaged me. Anyway, I am so happy that I got my car back," I said.

"Here. This is the place," he pointed out.

I parked the car and we went inside. It was a restaurant in Vijay Nagar. Amazing décor. Lovely ambience. Pleasant music. A perfect place to visit after a long tiring day.

I was looking at one of the drawings on the wallpaper after we had found a place to sit, when he said, "Avantika, what would you like to have?"

I checked out the menu. Earlier, whenever I visited any restaurant, Chinese and continental were my first priorities, but lately I had developed a certain kind of aversion towards the two. So I ordered a pizza.

"Nothing else?" he asked.

"No, sir."

"Why?" he asked.

"Just like that. It is enough for me."

"Okay. You can always order something later. What would you like to drink?"

I chose a drink for both of us as he wanted to have a drink of my choice. He placed the order and we settled down to chat.

"Avantika, I want to tell you something," he said.

His expression became grave. A certain fear gripped me. Was he going to tell me that it was over? That he would stop talking to me?

"I know that what we have between us cannot be called a relationship, per se. We don't talk for long hours. In fact, we don't even talk every day. Honestly, I had been trying to resist coming close to you till now. But now I can't do that anymore. I want to spend more time with you. I want to talk to you more often," he said.

"Don't get me wrong, Avantika. I don't want to take advantage of you. I don't want anything from you in return. It's just that I want to keep you happy because doing so would make me happy. I can't express how grateful I am for you being there with me. I want to buy you flowers, greet you as you open your eyes in the morning and close them at night, buy gifts for you and do everything I can to make you feel special," he added.

"I can understand. Every second I spend with you makes me realise how special I am. You don't have to buy flowers or gifts for me to make me feel special," I said.

"No, no, Avantika. I want to do these things for you. In fact, not entirely for you but for myself, for my satisfaction," he said.

"You can do whatever makes you happy. I just want to see you happy. I second your thoughts. I want to spend more time with you, too. In fact, I feel like hugging you whenever I see you in college but I wanted to give you some time to come to terms with everything that's going on between us," I said.

"You are the only person with whom I can share anything because I know you'll understand me," he said, holding my fingers.

"I am sorry if any of my words hurt you," I said.

"I know that I had been very rude that day. I called you a coward. I am really very sorry," I added.

"No, Avantika. You don't have to be sorry. In fact, I am sorry for acting so silly," he said.

"No, sir. It wasn't your fault." As I said this, the waiter came up with his order.

He had ordered a pizza too, but a different one. He shifted his plate to my side and asked me to eat. I said "no thanks" but he insisted. After a few minutes, the waiter arrived with my order.

"The food here is delicious!" I remarked.

"So bringing you here paid off," he said.

We both laughed. We didn't talk much while eating. While we were sipping our drinks, Mr. Joseph asked me about my birth date. When I asked about his, he said it was 5 March. I asked him how he celebrated it to which he answered that his birthdays weren't much exciting as most of his friends were either married or out of town, working. He was thankful if they even remembered to wish him as nobody had the time to do so nowadays. On being asked if he had a British origin, because of his accent, he answered in the negative, asserting that he was an Indian Christian from Bangalore. He added an interesting statement to this. He said that as he celebrated Christmas every year, he noticed that as he grew older, his Christmas list got smaller and the things he really wanted could no longer be bought. His words proclaimed a sad truth of life.

I had promised myself that I would make his birthday special as it was just round the corner; that I would do whatever it took to make him happy. I hated to see him sad.

"So what do you do after college?" I asked him.

"I read, watch movies, and attend events if there are any," he said.

"What will you do after we're done with lunch?" he asked.

"I have a meeting to attend," I replied.

"What meeting?" he asked.

"I have a meeting every Tuesday for *DU Times*," I answered.

"Oh! So when do you have to leave?" he asked.

"Around 3.15 p.m." I said.

"You have time," he said, looking at his watch.

Our drinks were over in a few minutes.

"Would you like to have some ice cream?" he asked.

"No, no. I've eaten a lot. I can't have anything now," I answered.

"Come on, Avantika. We'll share. We'll have a small one," he said.

"But…" I tried to make a point when he stopped me.

"You haven't even seen the quantity which they serve. It's a small cup and I'm asking you to share! So, no arguments."

I had to agree. After placing the order, he turned to me and said, "Till the time we finish eating it, it will be time for you to leave. It is the best thing we could do meanwhile."

"Did you like spending a few hours with me, Miss Sareen?" he asked.

"Of course, I did. It helped me to know you better," I said, with a smile on my face.

As the minutes passed, I was falling in love with him even more. Every microsecond that elapsed brought me closer to his being.

We shared a lot over the cup of ice-cream. Strawberry was the flavour we had chosen. He kept telling me that I ate like a bird due to the small bites I took to which I just laughed.

Goodbyes soon followed. I had a great time with him. Before leaving, I assured him that it was the best lunch that I ever had. I had promised myself that I would be there for him no matter how bad the situation was, that I would fulfil all his wishes no matter how many miles separated us, that my love for him was for eternity and beyond.

•

During the meeting, Anurag and I talked, for a change. He didn't talk to many people. He was selective. His charm was irresistible to everyone. I had never been attracted to a guy's voice before, but I guess I liked that about him. I had seen him after a long time, so we had a nice chat. I thought about him and what he said on my way back home and afterwards too. In fact, he was on my mind till it was night, even while I was chatting with Mr Joseph. His thoughts and views brought into motion a process of self-knowledge. In a way, he made me explore things about myself. If devoid of his voice and all the things that made him charming, Anurag would have had no effect on me, because I wouldn't have listened to him otherwise, like the others. This wasn't the case with Mr Joseph. He wasn't reduced to any set of special characteristics. He wasn't limited to his physical appearance or voice. For me, he was complete.

Since that day, Mr Joseph and I met regularly and had a chat every day. A message waited for me every day to be opened, wishing me 'Good morning, love' as soon as I opened my eyes. A message would mark the end of my day telling me to sleep carefree as all my problems could be solved by one man. We had exchanged each other's schedules so that we'd know when both of us would be free. We spent time with each other once every two days. Going for a walk around North Campus near the ridge, visiting restaurants, talking about our past relationships, our plans for the future, our first love affairs and their failures! Random discussions on news, frequent disagreements and arguments, making fun of each other's slips of tongue, fighting for our favourite actors, remembering how amazing school life used to be, sharing our bad experiences and sorrows. Every single act that we did together, every single sip of coffee we had together and every single word we uttered in the presence of each other helped in bringing us closer. The key to my happiness was in his pocket and that of his in mine. Neither of us had officially said the three magical words proclaiming our love for each other. Of course, they found a place in our messages and phone calls but never in person.

Nothing major had happened in college in the meantime. February was the season of fests in DU and all the fun and frolic was to begin after mid-February.

Time elapsed in the blink of an eye and 14 February's morning sun cast its light on earth. Mr Joseph hadn't wished me a 'Happy Valentine's Day' till then. Nor did I, thinking that the day held no significance for him. I was late for college that day. I was rushing towards the classroom. My eyes were fixed on my goal, which was the building where my class was supposed to take place. I was walking as fast as I could when suddenly someone came in my way.

"In a rush?" Keith sir inquired.

"Yes. I'm late for class. See you later. Bye," I hadn't even stopped moving while answering.

"Avantikaaaa…" I heard his voice as I surged ahead but couldn't stop. I was already late.

I was expecting to enter the class filled with students and Raghav sir teaching, but on the contrary, I could see students moving around the class with no professor in sight. Phew! Raghav sir hadn't arrived till then.

We waited for ten minutes but he didn't show up. Assuming that he wouldn't come, we dispersed. Almost everybody went to have coffee! I decided to go to Keith sir as he might have found my running away disrespectful.

I told my friends that I had to go to the library. As I was climbing down the stairs, I saw him coming up. On seeing each other, both of us stopped.

We said 'Hi' simultaneously and then smiled together.

"Weren't you supposed to be in a class right now?" he asked.

"It was Raghav sir's class. He hasn't come till now," I answered.

"Oh."

"I heard you calling out my name when I was in a rush," I said.

"Yes…umm…I wanted to ask you if you were free to go somewhere with me after your classes get over?" he said hesitatingly.

"Yes, sure," I replied.

"Great. Wait for me for ten minutes after your last class. I'll meet you at 1.00 p.m. okay?" he asked. "I've a workshop to attend," he added.

"Okay. No problem," I said with a smile.

"So, I will see you then. Have a nice time during classes," he winked.

"See you."

"Avantika!" he called out, when I had climbed down two steps.

"Happy Valentine's Day."

He wished me! It felt extremely good.

"I had been waiting for that since the past ten hours. Happy Valentine's Day to you too," I replied.

He laughed. We exchanged our goodbyes and went our respective ways.

I stood in front of the staff room at the decided time. He arrived five minutes later.

"Hi! I am so sorry you had to wait," he apologized as soon as he stood in front of me.

"It's okay. You don't have to apologize. Anyway, so where are we going?" I asked.

"To my place," he said.

It was an unexpected reply. I stood there with a blank face.

"Actually, I wanted to cook for you. It's okay if you are uncomfortable. We can go somewhere else…"

I didn't let him finish and said, "I have no problem in going to your place. Let's go."

He grinned and we left.

He lived on the second floor. It was a white building facing a lawn. I parked my car nearby. He opened the lock and we went inside. His flat had two bedrooms and one drawing room. On the right hand side, there was a kitchen and a bed room. On the left hand side, there was the other smaller bedroom. Everything was placed in an orderly fashion with all the things at their proper places, and the white walls impeccably clean.

"Is it generally so neat and tidy or have you made a special effort today?" I asked.

"What?" he asked back.

"Your house," I said.

"Special effort," he answered and laughed.

"Come, sit," he said.

I sat down on the sofa.

"I'll get some coffee for you."

Having said this, he began walking towards the kitchen.

He was making coffee when the doorbell rang. He went outside the house to deal with the person.

Why did he do that? That's very suspicious! Was the person threatening him?

He came inside and asked me to close my eyes.

A surprise?

I did the same. I could hear the door closing and the sound of plastic being touched. He asked me to open my eyes, as the sound faded away. I could make out from the intensity of his voice that he was near me. As I opened my eyes, I saw him sitting on his knees with a bouquet of red roses mixed with lilies. I was in awe. It was the perfect combination that he could have given to me.

"Thank you so much," I gushed.

"You like it?"

"I *love* it!" I said, emphasizing on the word in the middle.

"Happy Valentine's day," he said.

"Happy Valentine's day. God, I am so happy! I love you," I said.

I love you! I had finally said that in person!

"I love you too, Avantika," he said.

Was this a dream? Could this be real? I had never thought that he could be so romantic!

"Let me show what I've made for you. Till then, you may have the pleasure of sitting next to these flowers," he said, with a glimmer in his eyes.

I laughed, grinned, smiled all at once!

After a few minutes, he came out of the kitchen. I stood up and while taking a few steps towards him, I said, "Let me help you."

"No. Sit."

I didn't sit but stopped where I was.

"Please, Avantika. Sit," he reasserted.

Slowly, I sat down on the sofa.

It took him three rounds to place everything on the table. After presenting the food before me, he came and sat next to me.

"Oh my god! What was the need to make all this for me!" I exclaimed, looking at the number of dishes.

He laughed.

Noodles, pizza, garlic bread, rajma, rice, chapatis – made just for me!

"Oh god! Were you thinking that I'd be bringing my friends along?! I would have been happy with just a slice of toast. Were you cooking the whole night?" I reacted.

"Do you want toast? Wait, I'll get some," he said, while getting up.

"No! I don't want anything else. Sit down," I said.

"I was just trying to say that there was no need to do so much for me. Sit down now!" I added.

He sat down.

"Tell me how they taste," he said.

My plate was full without any space left for anything else, even though I had taken a small quantity of every dish.

As I tasted all the dishes, I praised him, "They are so delicious!"

"I can't believe it. You are such a good cook! Are you a part time chef, or have you borrowed the recipe from some really good chef? This is beyond perfection! Why don't you lend me your recipes?" I said.

He laughed.

"Thank you, Miss Sareen. So I'm not that bad at cooking?" he replied.

"Mr Joseph, you're amazing! I can get married to you because of this," I complimented him.

He laughed.

He asked me if I would like some music. I told him that his voice was the best music I had ever heard.

He gestured to me to start eating. Food was our topic of discussion while we gorged on the yummy dishes.

"Seriously, I had never thought that you could be so romantic and such a great cook!" I said, after we finished eating.

He laughed and said, "Thank you."

While leaving, I asked him if I could hug him for making the day so special for me. He agreed.

I hugged him and told him that it was the best Valentine's Day ever.

"Where will you keep the flowers?" he asked.

"In a vase," I answered.

"What will you tell your parents? Will they ask too many questions?"

"No, they won't. I'll tell my mother that an admirer has given them to me," I said, smiling.

He laughed and accompanied me downstairs.

"I hope you know the way or should I accompany you?" he asked.

"I know. Don't worry," I replied and left.

My mom questioned me about the flowers.

"A random guy. He likes me. I couldn't resist the flowers, so brought them along but I'm not dating anyone. You don't need to worry," I lied.

She laughed and said, "Well, whatever the case may be. The guy has an impressive taste when it comes to flowers."

We both laughed and placed the flowers in a vase.

I hated lying to my mom but it was the safest thing to do until the right time arrived.

•

We had our department fest on 16 February. Some guys from a fashion company had landed in our college in the morning. They were taking pictures for free, providing us with coloured wigs, big shades with weird shapes and many other accessories. I got myself photographed with heart-shaped shades and a rainbow coloured wig along with Ritvik, Anamika and Manvika.

We went to attend the talk by P. Sainath after that. I could see all the teachers of our department present at the talk except Keith sir. Not able to deal with his absence, I texted him asking him where he was. In reply, he said that he wasn't well so couldn't make it to the college. Leaving the talk in between, I called him. He told me that he was down with fever.

"What? Why didn't you tell me that you have fever when you texted me in the morning? How much is it?" I asked.

"Not much. Don't worry, I'll be fine," he replied vaguely.

"How. Much. Is. It?" I retaliated because of his reply.

"A hundred," he lied.

"Swear on me," I said.

"Okay, okay. I lied. A hundred and two," he said.

"I'm coming to your house," I disconnected the call without listening to his reply.

Ritvik had come outside too. I told him that I had some work and had to leave.

"But we were supposed to go to Kamla Nagar after the fest, right?" he asked.

"You can go with Anamika and Manvika. I am sorry but I will have to leave urgently," I answered and rushed towards the parking area.

After the talk, there was a creative writing competition and games like Wordpecker and treasure hunt. I was going to miss them.

I rang the doorbell of Mr Joseph's place and I was surprised to see him when he opened the door Dishevelled hair and unkempt looks made him look like a college boy.

"Anamika! Why did you come? You should attend the fest. It's your first department fest in college," he said.

"This is not how you invite people in!" I replied.

"Come in," he said, with a sigh.

"Why didn't you tell me that you weren't well? You should have told me. There is nobody with you. What if I do the same?

Not tell you when I'm unwell, I mean. How would you feel then?!" I let out my anger.

Seeing me getting agitated, he grabbed my shoulders and hugged me.

"I am okay. I am sorry. Relax," he whispered in my ears.

"Time to go back to bed," I told him.

"You had your breakfast?" I asked, while he lay down on the bed.

"Yes," he replied.

"Have you taken the medicines?" I questioned him.

"Yes," he answered.

"What did you have for breakfast?"

"Dal and rice."

"Okay. You should sleep. I am here. Tell me if you need anything," I said.

"Avantika, I'm alright. I can manage a situation like this. My maid will come in a few hours and she'll make something for me for lunch and dinner. You don't have to stay here. You can go back to college," he said.

"I'm staying," I asserted.

"You're missing out on all the fun."

"I still have the college fest to attend; this is just our department's I can have fun then."

He didn't say anything.

"I can't sleep. I've a headache," he said after a few minutes.

"Headache? Should I make something for you? Tea? Coffee?" I asked.

"You know how to make tea?"

"Yes. Wait, I'll be right back," I replied and went to make some tea.

"You know what I like the most about you?" he asked while sipping tea.

"What?" I asked back.

"That you are an amalgamation of a strong and a gentle woman. You assume the role of the former when you strongly feel that something is right and the latter when you are engaged with the people you love," he said.

I smiled and said, "You know I read somewhere that being a woman, one must think like a man, act like a lady, look like a young girl and work like a horse. You have to assume multiple identities. That's what the world demands."

He liked the tea and said that he was feeling better after drinking it. After some time, my phone rang. It was from a girl regarding the *DU Times*. I wondered if the excuse I had made to come to see Mr Joseph would eventually turn into the truth and that some work would be assigned to me. The call was intended to discuss some issues and went on for about twenty minutes. By the time I came back to Mr Joseph's room, he was asleep. I switched off the lights and sat beside him. I thought that I should wait at least till his maid arrives. Having nothing to do, I started reading the book which was kept on the side table. I had never heard the name of the author before, but after reading a few pages, I could tell that he was good.

When I looked at the clock next, it was 2.00 p.m. His maid hadn't come yet. He was still asleep. I went to the kitchen to check if there was anything he could eat for lunch. I could only see rice and some leftover dal. The quantity was too meagre for a proper meal. He should have something better to eat when he wakes up, I thought. I decided to cook something for him since it seemed that the maid wasn't coming anytime soon. I knew how to make matar paneer and shahi paneer, the only two dishes I wanted to learn how to cook. The last time I had shown interest in cooking was when I was with Aarav. Before starting, I checked if the ingredients were there in the kitchen. They were. I chose to make matar paneer and put some potatoes into it.

I cut the potatoes and the cottage cheese into pieces. There were frozen peas in the fridge. I searched for the mixer grinder and the tomato paste was ready in a jiffy once I found it. I cooked the food with utmost sincerity. It took me an hour or so for the whole process. I had tasted the poor dish a zillion times to make sure that it was good. After that, it struck me that I'd have to make some chapatis too. I went to check on Mr Joseph before starting the next job. He had not woken up. It took me fifteen minutes to find the flour and fifteen more to make nine chapatis. I didn't know how many to make, so I made four for lunch and dinner each and an extra. I wrapped them in aliminium foil to keep them warm and went to check on him again. He had not moved an inch. Fearing that he may be lying unconscious, I tried to tickle him. He moved. Thank god!

I read a few more pages and when the clock struck four, I started receiving messages from my dad asking me when I'd be home. The fest helped me cover up for the delay. I told him that I would be leaving after half an hour. I couldn't concentrate on the book anymore. I went to check if there were any fruits in the refrigerator. There weren't. I took out an orange from my bag and kept it on one of the side tables in the room where Mr Joseph was sleeping. I kept a note under it.

"I checked your refrigerator. There were no fruits. You need to eat them to get well soon, so I am keeping one here.

Please eat it. I've also made lunch and dinner. Yes, I know you can take care of yourself, but I was doing it for myself. The food isn't as delicious as you would make, but you could still try eating it. Text me when you wake up – Avantika."

I left his house at 4.30 p.m. In the evening, I received a message from Mr Joseph.

Thank you so much for what you did! The food is good. Fairly good attempt, Miss Sareen. I'll eat the orange, don't worry. Lots of love.

I inquired about his health after reading the message. He was feeling better than before.

He didn't come to college for the next two days. I would ask him if I should come over but he would say no, telling me that I should attend classes and assuring me that he was alright and would call me if he needed help. I had no option but to agree, but I still went there one day, though for only fifteen minutes, to deliver some fruits.

Fun and Frolic

It was 26 February, the first day of our college fest. The fest was a three-day event. There were competitions like the battle of bands, music, writing, photography and others to be held on that day. I didn't take part in any of them. I wanted to participate in the creative writing one but it was the concluding day of Hans Raj College's fest and I had to make a report on the same for the *DU Times*. I took Manvika and Anamika along. Ritvik was a part of the dance team so he couldn't accompany us. It was the day of the concert in Hans Raj – a live performance by Mohit Chauhan. There were many events like the inter-college dance competition, fashion show, treasure hunt and some informal games. We witnessed each of them for some time and attended the concert for about forty-five minutes. We enjoyed the concert and got the results of all competitions from the respective supervisors.

Competitions like treasure hunt, face painting, rangoli making, basketball were held on the second day of our college fest which were followed by the Sufi Night. Unfortunately, I couldn't stay too long for the Sufi Night, the only event which took place in the evening as my parents didn't want me to drive home alone late at night. I couldn't stay back with my friends who lived as paying guests because of permission issues.

KK was the star to perform on the third day of the fest – the day everyone was waiting for. Not disappointing us, he sang some of his best songs for us and built an enchanting atmosphere. There wasn't a single person who wasn't mesmerized by his voice. The day was insane, unforgettable, full of fun and truly displayed what college life should be like.

●

I had not met Mr Joseph in those three days, but we were in contact. We met on 1 March but only for a short span of time as it was the concluding day of the SRCC fest and Sonu Nigam was supposed to begin his performance at 4.00 p.m. My girlfriends and I wanted to attend it. We reached SRCC at 3.00 p.m. and waited for forty-five minutes after which it was announced that the singer was running late due to some reasons and was expected to arrive at 8.00 p.m. It was impossible for Anamika and me to attend the concert that late in the night, so we left in two hours. Events like paper dance and other competitions went on while the crowd was told to wait till the singer arrived.

I was really disappointed. I could've attended it for, like, twenty minutes or so, I kept telling my mother. However, there was some consolation when I came to know that he had arrived at nine and the concert had ended earlier than expected. Many people had left by that time. I heaved a sigh of relief knowing that I wasn't the only one who missed it. It gave me a sense of comfort.

The next major thing in my life was Mr Joseph's birthday. I wanted to give him the whole world that day so that he would have no wishes unfulfilled. His birthday was on a Sunday. I had thought of different ways to surprise him but before finalizing anything, I wanted to make sure that he had no other plans.

On 2 March, when we met after classes and sat down on our favourite seating wall in the parking area, I asked about his birthday plans. He said that he might go out.

"With whom?" I asked.

"With someone of the opposite sex," he said, giving out a mischievous smile.

"And who is that?" I questioned him.

"I call her Miss Sareen," he answered.

I sighed and he laughed.

"You know, I would really like to take you somewhere. To a specific 'somewhere' actually," he said.

"Where?" I asked.

"That's a surprise."

"A surprise? But isn't it your birthday? I am supposed to give surprises, not you,"

"It doesn't matter," he said.

"But I wanted to give you a surprise," I said, with a sad face.

"Avantika, I haven't shown that place to many people. I wanted to go there with you on a special occasion. I can't wait any longer. Please come," he said.

"What I want is your happiness, no matter how. I'll come with you," I answered.

Hearing this, his face lit up.

"Great! So I'm going to pick you up from your house, take you there and spend time with you. The perfect birthday plan!" he said, happily.

"Now, why are you picking me up? It is your birthday!! I'll come to your house and we can go wherever you want us to go," I answered.

"No, I'll pick you up. I don't want you to drive. And picking you up will add a cherry to my cake of happiness," he said.

"Why don't you want me to drive?" I asked, curiously.

"Firstly, the place is far off. Secondly, I don't want you to be busy driving. I want you to feel free. Thirdly, we always travel in your car and I want to make my birthday a little different. And most importantly, we might get late while coming back. I don't want you to travel alone in that case. I want to drop you at your house safe and sound, for my satisfaction," he explained.

"Yes, sir," I said, saluting him.

He laughed.

So, before I could finalise my plan, he had already finalised his. To me, it seemed as though it was my birthday instead of his, but I had the satisfaction that it would ultimately lead to his happiness. I was really excited about his birthday, waiting to go to the place he was so eager to take me to.

I prepared small surprises for him as I too wanted to do something for him.

Destiny

The preparations for Keith sir's birthday had taken off from 3 March. On that day, I went to the market, bought boxes of different sizes, light blue and green chart paper, a Tommy Hilfiger watch and ingredients to bake a cake. I wrapped up the boxes with the chart paper making five boxes of blue and green colour. I made a layered gift, putting the smaller boxes inside the bigger ones, such that the smallest one contained the watch. And then, I wrapped the outer biggest box like a gift. Having done this, I was so exhausted that I immediately dozed off to sleep.

I didn't meet Mr Joseph the next day as I had to reach home early. With the help of my mom and websites, I baked a cake for my dear professor, making my mother live under the illusion that it was for my friend's birthday. After putting the cake in the oven, I sat down to write a poem for him. He was the second person for whom I was doing that. I faired out the poem on a light green chart paper using markers.

As the clock struck twelve, I wished the man I truly respected for being what he was, a 'Happy Birthday'. We decided the time when he would pick me up and the place from where he would do that. Picking up from home was not the wisest choice, obviously.

I couldn't sleep properly at night due to my apprehension regarding the next day. I was worried and hoped everything would go on as we had planned.

I had slept only for three hours. I got out of my bed at 8.00 a.m. I went to the kitchen to write 'Happy Birthday' on the cake with cream. My mom was already working in the kitchen. She asked me the reason for waking up so early on a Sunday. I reminded her that I had a birthday party to attend. I had told her the previous day that I would leave in the morning and one of my friends would pick me up from so and so place. I added that I could be late while coming back and she needn't worry about that as one of my friends who lived nearby, would be accompanying me. I didn't write Keith sir's name on the cake lest my mom spotted it. When my mom asked me as to why there wasn't any name, I told her that there was no space on the cake since my friend had a long name.

After that, I sent a 'Good Morning' message to Mr Joseph and he reminded me that he was coming at 11.00 a.m. sharp. I took a shower, had breakfast and repeated the story of friend's birthday to my dad, word to word. It was 9.30 a.m. now. I took a final look at the gifts and put them inside a poly bag.

At 10.45 a.m., I was ready to go out with the most amazing professor I had ever met. I had put on a red dress, accessorized myself and applied a little make-up. I texted him and asked about his whereabouts when I was ready. He said that he would arrive in twenty minutes. After minutes of anticipation, my phone rang. It was him, asking me to come outside, on the back side of the park which was closest to my house – our rendezvous point.

The park was about a hundred metres from my house, but I knew it would seem like a mile walking in my favourite pair of heels. After taking one final look at myself in the mirror, when I was rushing towards the door of my house, I heard my mom calling me from behind.

"Won't you take this along?" she asked, pointing towards the tray in her hand. It was the cake!

"Oh god. How could I forget that!" I exclaimed.

"Wait. I'll put it in a box," she said, smiling.

"Mom! My saviour!" I said.

"Miss Sareen, I thought you were ready!" said Mr Joseph as I answered the phone on my way to the park.

"I'm on my way," I replied.

Answering the phone when both of my hands were occupied was a tough task so I declined the offer to keep talking till I reached his car.

As I came closer to the park, I could see a white Honda Civic parked at an irregular angle as compared to the rest of the cars. I knew it was him.

"Oh my god! What have you brought?" he asked, on seeing my hands being full.

The cake was in my left hand, while the right had the gift and my cell phone.

He took the poly bag from me so I could sit down. He was occupying the back seat of the car while a driver occupied the driver's seat. The car started moving as soon as I closed the door, without any instructions being given by Mr Joseph.

"Do you want me to open these?" he asked, while I was dialling my mom's number to let her know that I had met my 'friend'.

I asked him to stay quiet. After I disconnected the call, he repeated the question to which I answered,

"Your wish."

"Hmm.. I'll open them when we reach our destination," he said. I smiled.

He started typing something on his phone. Two minutes later, I received a message. It was Keith sir.

I hope you don't mind the presence of the driver. Sorry for the lack of privacy. I find driving uncomfortable. But don't worry, he's a good guy.

I am fine with it. Don't worry.

"So, did you sleep last night?" I asked him.

"Yes, I did. I received calls till 1.00 a.m. and slept afterwards."

"Cool. So are you going to tell me now, where are we heading?"

"Not yet, Miss Sareen," he answered, raising his right eyebrow.

I tried imitating me but couldn't raise my eyebrow. He laughed.

"Not that you'll tell me but still, what have you brought for me?" he asked.

"Lips are sealed," I replied.

He laughed.

"You're looking gorgeous, Miss Sareen," he complimented me.

"Thank you, Mr Joseph." I replied. "You are looking handsome too."

He was wearing a full sleeved black T-shirt with blue jeans. Everything about his looks was same as that in college.

After minutes of looking out of the window, he put the poly bags lying between us aside and while holding my right hand, he said, "I'm glad that you came."

His eyes were shining with a mystical energy I had never seen before.

We chatted with each other throughout the journey, without caring about the distance that separated us from our destination.

When the driver told us that we had reached, we were in shock. Being oblivious of our surroundings, we didn't realize how or when the time passed. Mr Joseph insisted to hold both the bags but choosing not to do as he was saying, I held onto the cake while he held the other. The first thing I noticed after we got out of the car was a board that read 'Joseph Farms'.

"Is this your farmhouse?" I asked the birthday boy as we moved towards the gate.

"Yes. When we lived in Bangalore, it served as our family's picnic spot," he said, cheerfully. I smiled.

The security guard gave him a salute and we went inside.

All I could see on the west side were trees, plants, flowers, and greenery, while the east side had a swing, lemon plants, and mango trees with squirrels running around all over the grounds. Vibrant blues, yellows and reds shone in the clusters of flowers. I was mesmerized by the entwined ivy that snaked up the side of the marble wall of imposing height. Never in my life had I seen grass so green. Walking towards the straight path marked by tiles, leading to the house, we crossed two trees bent towards each other, creating an arch. Several vines and rose bushes lined the house's exterior.

He held my right hand as we walked inside the house. It was marvellous. The lights were already on. The house was shining. The light from the chandelier gave out pleasant reflections and the soft breeze made the wind chimes produce a soothing music. The windows had perfect arches.

The walls were covered in artwork that looked like they were from a museum. The marble floor was spotless and looked like no one had ever walked on it and the hallway seemed never-ending.

We took a round around the house. Every room had a high roof. The kitchen was as big as the drawing room. The crockery was already out on the dining table with a knife and other utensils. Everything was covered with fine linen. The view was breathtaking.

"Mr Joseph, this place is a paradise. If there is heaven, I'm sure it looks like this place," I said.

He laughed.

I was so lost in the world of 'fantasy-turned-reality' that I had not even realised when Mr Joseph had taken the bag from my hand and placed it on the table, along with the rest of the stuff.

"I am glad you brought me here. I could have never shown you a place as beautiful as this one," I said.

"I keep coming here. Gives me solace. In fact, I would love to live here permanently. It's just the distance from college that's keeping me from doing that," he said.

I smiled.

A man clad in white came to us with glasses of water. I told him that I didn't want it, and Mr Joseph did the same. He went away, keeping the tray on the table.

"You know, this place suits you. You already look like a princess and this place, your palace," Mr Joseph showered praises on me.

"And you are my prince, aren't you?" I smirked at him.

He laughed and replied, "Very well, Miss Sareen."

As he said this, a woman arrived and asked us if we

would like to have tea or coffee. I replied in the negative but Mr Joseph asked her to bring two cups of coffee.

"Sit, Miss Sareen," he said.

We sat on the sofa next to each other.

"Let me open your gifts now!" he said, rubbing his hands.

He took out the box from one of the poly bags, unwrapped it, opened it and found another box. He opened the second box and found a third. He opened the third and found a fourth! I couldn't conceal my laughter. Seeing his face made me laugh. The delay was making him all the more impatient. He was laughing too.

"Miss Sareen, so much suspense! Am I going to find some treasure in the end?" he joked.

He opened the fourth and there was a fifth. He opened the fifth and there was a sixth. I was laughing so hard that my stomach began to hurt.

"Keep laughing! Are you making a fool out of me?" he commented.

He continued his exercise of opening the boxes till he reached the tenth one.

"Okay now. If I find another box, I am not going to open it," he said.

He opened the box and took out the watch.

"Though there was another box. The watch box. I still opened it, you see," he said.

"I love the watch, Miss Sareen. I am amazed to see that you knew what I'd like," he added, after wearing the watch.

I smiled and said, "I know you far better than you think I do."

He then caught hold of the next poly bag and found the poem which I had written for him. He read it. It was as if he was lost in the depth of the words. He was completely focussed.

"Oh my god! This is so touching. It's like all your feelings have been laid bare before me."

He said and hugged me.

"I love you, Avantika. I love you so much. This is the most precious gift I've ever received."

He said, while we were still hugging each other, "You know, I don't want to push you away, but I am dying to open the next box," he added.

I laughed.

He opened the box which had the cake.

"Did you make it?" he asked. I nodded.

He was about to take a bite when I stopped him.

"No. You got to cut it first," I said.

"Oh god! I'm already craving for it," he replied.

I laughed. I had brought candles along. We placed the candles on the cake.

"I'm sorry I didn't write your name. Mom would've noticed it so…" I apologised to him.

"I understand, Avantika," he said and kissed me on the forehead.

He asked someone to bring a match box. Meanwhile, we placed the cake on the dining table.

After lighting the candles, I asked him to call all his helpers and all of us sang the birthday song while he cut the cake. He put the first big piece in my mouth and I returned the gesture. The servants got back to their work after wishing him.

"Did you like it? Is it bad? Pathetic?" I asked Mr Joseph.

He remained silent. On seeing him quiet, I said, "Okay. I won't bake a cake ever again."

He pulled me towards himself, looked into my eyes and said, "No confectionary shop could've provided me with a cake as luscious as this."

My face lightened up and I hugged him.

"And don't think that I am praising you to make you happy. Every person who'll taste it will say the same," he added.

I smiled.

"Now, my love, let us eat something first and then, we'll do whatever you want," he said, putting his arms on my shoulder. I nodded.

He ordered for the food to be brought out. Meanwhile, he ate half of the cake.

"Did you take anybody's help?" he asked, pointing towards the cake.

"Yes. I didn't know how to make it. Mom and Google helped," I answered. He laughed.

Italian and Chinese food was put on the table. The food was good, but wasn't made by him this time. By the time we finished eating, it was 2.30 p.m.

After lunch, we walked through his gardens. We walked hand in hand while I rested my head on his arm. There were exquisite varieties of flowers; we played with the birds while we fed them together. We sat on the swing and talked about numerous things, from the black and orange striped butterfly that sat on the white flowers to small kids to countries to the stars – everything. While talking about small kids, he told me something that he had read somewhere. He told me that we should always smile at little children because not doing so would weaken their faith in humanity and goodness.

After spending time amidst nature, we went inside. He played soft music and danced together. He taught me how to make donuts. Learning had never been so much fun. I played with his hair, he played with mine. We teased each other. As the evening approached, we escaped into the garden once more. He caught the best butterflies for me, by making them sit on his hands. We ate ice-cream watching the sunset. The lights in the garden illuminated our path and kept us from stepping on squirrels. I could wait for an eternity to spend a day like that with him again. In each other's company, we were complete, like two incomplete halves fused into one. I had experienced life at its best, with him. He was the perfect man for me.

Soon it was time to get back to our normal lives.

"Avantika, we should leave now. It'll take time to reach your home," he said, while we sat on the swing.

He hugged me for one last time.

"I never wanted the day to end, Avantika, but time doesn't move according to our will," he said.

He gave me a peck on the forehead and I hugged him even tighter.

"I don't want to go," I said.

He laughed and said, "Don't worry. I'll make every day as special as today."

He took the box containing the cake and the chart paper with the poem written on it along, as we walked towards the car. He was already wearing the watch I gave him.

"I'll eat this cake at night," he said.

I laughed and we got inside the car.

"Thank you for making my birthday so special," he said.

"The pleasure was all mine, Mr Joseph," I replied.

It was 7.30 p.m. when we left his farmhouse. On being asked if he would go home after dropping me, he said that he would go to an orphanage first as he donated some money every year on his birthday. He was keen on doing something for children and contributing some money for their betterment made him feel good. He told me about the orphanage. I told him that he could do that the next day as it was late but he said that he wouldn't be at peace until he did so.

We reached my house at 8.30 p.m. He dropped me a few metres away from my house. He looked at me and told me that he would meet me in college as he shook hands with me. As I withdrew my hands, a strange feeling seized me. I felt as if a phase was coming to an end, as if my life would never be the same when I get out of the car, as if I was leaving a part of myself in the car.

I told my mom that I wouldn't be having dinner and headed to my room. She asked me about the party and I told her that it was the best party I had ever attended. She asked me what was so special about it. I told her that I was tired and would tell her everything the next day. I needed time to make up a story! I went inside my room and changed my clothes. I lay down on the bed to relax, resisting the temptation to call him. Around 9.45 p.m., when I could no longer control myself, I called him. He seemed happy, very happy to be precise. He had left the orphanage just then and was in the car, going home. He told me that everyone at the orphanage greeted him politely even though he had gone there so late. Everybody knew him and they loved him. They had been waiting for him since morning and asked him to stay there for the night, but he said he had to go to the college the next day. He promised me that he would take me there one day and told me that he would talk to me after he reached home. I told him to text me as soon as he reached home and that was the end of our conversation.

Half an hour passed, but I received no message from him. After another fifteen minutes, I texted him about his whereabouts. The message was not delivered. I waited for the message to get delivered for fifteen minutes, but it did not. At 10.45 p.m., I called him. His number wasn't reachable. I was worried. He shouldn't have taken so much time to reach home from the orphanage. I tried his number again, but in vain. I kept trying his number till midnight and left several messages. I waited for his response the whole night. I wanted the night to pass quickly so that I could see him in college in the morning and know that he was alright.

He didn't come to deliver the lecture the next day. As soon as all the classes got over, I rushed out of the room. I had decided that I would go to his flat to check on him but before that, I went to see if he was there in the staff room, thinking that he might have come late. He wasn't there. As I got out of the room, I saw Raghav sir coming from a distance. I walked towards him.

"Good Afternoon, sir. Sir, have you seen Keith sir?" I asked him.

He didn't reply and started walking away from me.

"Sir!" I called him.

He stopped. I stood in front of him and asked him what the matter was.

"You were his favourite student, weren't you?" he asked. He was making a lot of effort to speak.

"I still am, sir. But what happened?" I asked.

"I want to meet him, sir. Please tell me where is he?" I added as he had not answered my previous question.

"I... I... I don't know what to say," he said with a choking voice.

"Why? What happened? Where is he?" I asked hastily.

"He's dead," he replied. Tears rolled down his cheeks as he said this.

His words echoed in my ears. I took a step back. My whole world had fallen apart. I had received a blow.

"What? How could you say that? He's alright. You think it's a joke? He was as well as any other person till yesterday," I started crying.

"He's dead, Avantika. He's dead," he sobbed.

"It is hard for us to believe this news too. An hour back, some policemen came to our college. They met the principal and told him that they had found his body lying on the road near the Red Fort, near the bridge from where the train passes. The principal called the staff of our department and broke the news to us. He…he was bleeding. He was hit badly. There were marks on his body. The police got his college card from his wallet. We didn't know how to tell you people about this…"

He broke down as he walked away.

I was numb, shattered, broken. I couldn't believe what I had just heard, but I knew that it was true. I couldn't think about anything. Raghav sir's words kept echoing in my ears. I wanted to run away from reality. I wanted to cry as loud as I could. How could that happen! It was his birthday yesterday! Tears kept flowing through my eyes. Everything was still. I had grown oblivious to my surroundings. I couldn't hear anything except the echo of his words. I was lost. I walked slowly towards my car. I broke down while driving. I cried and shouted as loudly as I could. My vision had blurred due to tears. I didn't know how, but I reached home. I had not heard the noise of the traffic on my way. I wasn't conscious of the directions, either. I was driving mechanically, like a machine programmed to take turns after specific points.

I went to my room and locked it from inside. My mom knocked on my door, shouting my name but I was deaf to everything. Nothing mattered to me. I kept weeping, crying, sobbing. I kept wishing it was a dream. I tried Keith sir's phone again... and again.. hoping that he would answer. But people don't pick up calls when they are dead.

I heard my mom crying. She was asking me to open the door. I didn't know for how long I made her suffer like that. But I knew that it was for quite some time when she hugged me tightly as soon as I opened the door. I kept weeping and she kept asking the reason for the same. I didn't know when I slept. When I woke up, it was 8.00 p.m. I was alone in my room and a sheet was over me. I didn't get out of my room, and didn't have the strength to do so either. I kept lying on the bed and tears filled my eyes once again. Mom came to my room and asked me to eat something. I refused. She kept my dinner on the side table and I asked her to leave me alone. She did as I said. I got up and bolted the door of my room. I didn't touch the food and stared listlessly at the wall.

I didn't want to go to college the next day, but I did during the break time to gather any information that might have reached Raghav sir. I met him. He had nothing to tell me except that Keith sir's sister had been contacted the day before and she was coming to college the day after to complete some formalities. I took Raghav sir's number and told him to give me any information he receives. Knowing that the students knew about Keith sir's death and not having the courage to face anyone, I headed back home. Anamika, Manvika and Ritvik had left a zillion messages on my phone, asking me where I was, informing me about my Keith sir's death and other stuff. I didn't take any calls. Nor did I reply to any message.

I didn't talk to anyone, not even to my mom who was the closest to me. I ate lunch after she had begged me to do so almost a hundred times. I felt bad for her, for being a parent to a child who was destined to be alone, for caring for a girl who was in so much pain herself that she couldn't feel her mother's, for loving a person who had lost everything including her heart, for hugging a body which was completely numb.

Everything made sense now. All those dreams which I had been having were a sign of the barrenness that lurked behind the plenitude of love. The red and white building was the Red Fort, the monument near which I lost my love. The darkness which engulfed the man of my dreams was the impending death. I was repelled by the darkness, destined as I was to live a solitary life of pain, loneliness and anguish. And the man was Keith sir.

The Fall of Humanity

The next day, I went to college in the morning but didn't attend classes. I sat in the college garden. I had pleaded to Raghav sir to text me when Keith sir's sister arrived. I really wanted to meet her. She was the reason why I was in college that day. Raghav sir had agreed. He must have sensed that there was something between Keith sir and me, but I didn't care. I kept taking rounds of the staff room after every half an hour, in case Raghav sir forgot to text me.

It was 11.30 a.m. I was on my way to the staff room when I received a text from Raghav sir, informing me that she had arrived. I hurtled past everyone. When I reached the staff room, she was talking to the teachers. I looked at her and knew that she was his sister. I stood in a corner and waited for her to end her conversation. She seemed extremely sad, as if she could cry any minute. She was fair, tall and slim. Her black hair was straight. She was wearing a full sleeved kurti with jeans. Everybody was telling her how great her brother was. They shared her grief. The female teachers hugged her while the men shook hands with her, offering their condolences. I couldn't see Raghav sir around. Perhaps he was too overwhelmed to talk to her.

When she had talked to everybody around and turned to leave, I walked up to her and asked her if she could talk to me for a few minutes. She agreed. I could feel a lump in my throat and in hers, too. I took her into the garden where I had taken refuge since morning. I asked her to sit but she refused.

"I'm Avantika. I was Keith sir's student and he was my favourite professor. He had told me about you and so I wanted to meet you," I could only manage to say this, initially.

She said, "Nice meeting you, Avantika. I am glad my brother had such good-hearted students."

I asked, "Can you please tell me what happened? I know that recalling the incident will be painful. But please. Can you?"

She closed her eyes for a few seconds, took a deep breath and looked at me. Tears had managed to escape my eyes by then. On seeing me crying, she hugged me and both of us sat on the seating wall. When my tears had stopped, she got up, looked away from me and started narrating the whole story which she had gathered from the police.

"The police says that he was probably travelling in a cab as no car was found around the place. He was passing by the Red Fort, near the bridge, when he saw three men attacking four people in a car. It was a family – a man with his wife and two children, a boy and a girl. The young girl was caught by one of them. He was molesting her while the other two were busy beating the rest of the family. The lady offered all her jewels and begged to let them go. Seeing the family pleading for their lives boosted their confidence. Keith saw this from the car he was travelling in and called the police immediately. He told the police about the incident that was taking place and added that he was a passerby. As soon as the police got to know, they left for the place. But he decided to intervene till the police arrived. The police think that he must have asked the driver to stop the car and he must have refused. Undeterred by the driver's refusal to intervene, he decided to leave the car and go on by himself. As he got into the fight, the family got a chance to escape but the girl, who was being molested, was still in the clutches of one of the men. Unconcerned about the girl, the rest of the family must have escaped in their car, leaving the girl behind. Keith was beaten by rods, hockey sticks and his body was stabbed many times with a knife. The girl, too, was beaten but not badly. Both the girl and Keith lay on the road. The attackers ran away as they had pacified their anger by beating him badly and most probably because they didn't want to get caught. Both of them were only half conscious. The girl saw a man coming to them but couldn't figure out his face. Keith asked him to take out the mobile from his pocket and make a call. He took out the mobile, but instead of calling an ambulance, he ran away with the mobile. That's the last thing that the girl saw. When the police reached the place, both the girl and Keith were unconscious. On being taken to the hospital, Keith was declared dead."

I was in a state of shock. I didn't know what to say. I could imagine everything happening in front of me as she narrated the incident. She turned towards me. She was crying. She called my name but I didn't answer. She sat by my side and held my hand. I hugged her and we cried together.

"How can people be so inhuman! That man left him dying for…for a phone…Just a phone! And that family! He was helping them...cowards! They left their daughter behind!" I sobbed.

She was crying with me, but was also a pillar of support for me. She wiped her tears and said, "She was not their real daughter. They had adopter her. The girl told the police that she used to live with lots of children earlier and some ladies took care of them. She was an orphan. The family was too concerned about saving their 'real blood'."

"Where is the girl now? How is she?" I asked.

"She's recovering in the hospital. She will be discharged and sent to an orphanage in a day or two," she answered.

"The police is trying to locate the orphanage in which she stayed earlier so that they can reach out to the people who had adopted her. They could help in finding out the people who attacked them," she added.

"But couldn't the girl provide any clue?" I inquired.

"Nothing substantial," she replied.

"You know, Keith always wanted to do everything he could for small children. He even wanted to adopt a child in case he didn't marry. Seeing the girl helpless must have stirred emotions in him and compelled him to do something about it. I know that not doing anything would've made him feel guilty. He would've never been able to look at himself in the mirror. He just paid the price of being too 'him'," she added and burst out crying.

I wiped her tears and said, "Your brother had the most beautiful soul. He was not made for this cruel, insensitive, callous world. He deserved better. Please don't cry. I know what you're going through. I am with you, no matter what. He will get justice. He will."

She wiped her tears.

"The car in which he was travelling was a Honda Civic. It was white in colour. I didn't take a note of the number. I didn't even look at the driver closely, but I have a faint idea about how he looked. If anything related to the driver can help in this case, please let me know," I said.

"That driver won't be of any help. We need to reach out to the family," she replied.

"I know and we will," I consoled her.

I asked for her number and she readily agreed to give it to me. I texted her my number so that she could contact me anytime she wanted to. She said that she had a few things to do in Delhi after which she would go back home. I asked her to keep me informed about the case and she agreed. She was a good person, like her brother. Before she left, we hugged each other and she said that she was glad to have met me. I said the same.

She did not ask how I knew about the car her brother was travelling in. I didn't tell her anything either. She must have assumed that I might have seen him around in that car that day or she might have been just too numb with grief and sorrow to give it another thought.

Reports relating to the incident found their way in the national newspapers. Mr Joseph was praised for his bravery and the police was pressurized to search for the attackers. *DU Times* covered the news too and I was made the in-charge. Two days after I had met Keith sir's sister, the man who had adopted the girl, visited a police station to inquire about her. The police caught hold of him and his family. Through sketches and other information, the three men were arrested and sent to prison, within a span of thirty days. I got all this information from the newspapers and Keith sir's sister confirmed it.

I never told my mother about my relationship with Mr Joseph and the reason for my changed behaviour. She didn't pressurize me either. Nobody knew about our story. It was engraved in my heart and was there to stay. I was proud of loving a man as great as Keith sir. I knew that as he sat in heaven, he watched me every day. I knew he never went away and watched me as I slept. He placed his arms around me as I wept. He saw me begging to god to return him to me. As long as his love was with me, I wasn't alone. I was guilty of not being there with him. But he knew that every breath I took, I was taking it for him.

Life Afterwards

For me, everything had changed since the incident. I was a more mature individual and it was no longer easy to make me laugh.

I was in the third year of college. I had made a silent promise to myself that I would be living to fulfil the tasks which were left incomplete by Mr Joseph. I avoided going out with my friends and liked to stay at home. I behaved normally except that I laughed less. My friends were the same. I still shared everything with my mother. I had started working for an NGO. I taught small children and found peace in teaching them. I visited the orphanage to which Mr Joseph donated money, once in every six months. I donated money to that orphanage on 5 March and took a pledge that I would do it every year, as long as I lived. I had told my parents that I would be opening an orphanage after being done with my studies, and they agreed to support me.

One day, our NGO decided to visit an orphanage and provide a special teaching session to the children there. Different teachers taught different subjects. While I was teaching, I saw a child. I had seen her photograph in the newspapers. After I finished teaching, I went to her and asked her name. It was her, the girl whom Mr Joseph had saved. I hugged her tightly. I took out Mr Joseph's photograph from my bag and asked her if she remembered him. She nodded and hugged me. Tears pooled in our eyes.

Suddenly, a man came and took the photograph from me. I got up and snatched it from him. I asked him who he was.

"Who are you?" he asked back.

"Why did you take the photograph from my hand? How dare you!" I replied.

"How do you know him?" he asked.

"If you know him, then you must also know about the circumstances which led to his death," he added, since I had not given any response to his previous question.

"Yes…but who are you?" I asked. My voice had softened.

"I'm the one whose family he had saved," he answered.

I stood there, shocked.

"You are that man! You disgusting piece of shit! How dare you touch his photograph! You coward! It was because of you and your family that he got into that fight and you people ran away. What are you doing here?! Get out of here. Get out, I said," I shouted at him.

"Listen to me. I am sorry for whatever happened. I know I shouldn't have run away but everything I did was to save my family. How could I see my wife and son suffering? I know I was wrong. I shouldn't have left my girl," as he said this, I cut him short.

"Your girl? She's not your girl!" I shouted.

"I know I don't deserve to be called her parent. That's why I never took her along with me, after that incident. I come to meet her from time to time. It gives me a sense of relief. These people can take care of her better than me. And perhaps, some day she will get the best parents in the world."

He continued, "But that day, I did come back. My conscience pricked me and I came back to the place after dropping my wife and son at a safe place. I took out the phone from the man's pocket and…"

"And? And did what? Ran away with the phone? You are such a disgusting person! Instead of helping him, you ran away with his phone. I don't want to see your face. I hope you rot in hell!" I shouted.

"No, I didn't. When I took out the phone, it was all broken. It wasn't working. I had gone to ask for help," he replied.

While we were talking, one of the ladies had taken the girl with her. I had no reason to stay and talk to the man. I started walking away from him.

"Hey! Who are you? How are you related to him? Hey!" he kept calling me but I didn't look back.

I had no specific word that would describe our relationship. We weren't just a professor and a student or boyfriend and girlfriend. Our relationship was neither bound by words nor by mortality of the flesh. We were two souls who admired, respected, loved, lived and breathed for each other. Time and space couldn't bind our relationship. It existed even when he was dead. It wasn't at a physical level but at a spiritual one. It transcended the rules of the society and of the world. Our souls were ready to meet each other in heaven. My life was all about completing his tasks, to do what he would have done and my final destination was to meet him, not in this world but the other one!

I didn't want to look for happiness in every passing moment anymore. I was tired of doing this ever since I took my first breath. I wanted those moments of joy to come by themselves – to knock the doors of my destiny and demand a little space by sadness' side. But somewhere deep down, I knew that happiness was, perhaps, too scared to ask and sadness too proud to adjust.

I was supposed to fight throughout my life. I figured that much. And that, after moments of breaking down, when I will gather myself and put together all those broken pieces and decide to fight again, the next blow will be even stronger. But I had this courage and strength inside me that I never had before, to withstand and fight back, to persevere, to go on – not just for my sake but for the people who loved me and looked up to me – and to go beyond the limits, for my determination was now stronger than ever.